ENLIGHTENMENT CLUB

by

Chris West

"Quiet people have the loudest minds."
Stephen Hawking

Copyright © Chris West 2024
Published by CWTK Publications
Cover photo by Alan Budman / Dreamstime
Cover design by Blondesign

Longing

There she is! The heroine of this narrative. The star. The centre!

A plain, chubby girl with glasses, hair that *will not* behave, and a sensible outfit – sensible apart from some bright orange platform boots that pinch at her feet and a genuine artist's beret (well, that's what the guy on Lewisham market said). She is standing in front of the archway that leads into the old Technical Institute, now turned Polytechnic of the South Circular. The inscription above it is still legible, despite a century of soot having been deposited on it:

KNOWLEDGE FOR ALL.

She feels a lump in her throat. This might be thanks to the *Gauloises* she has recently started smoking, but it's more than that. It's excitement. OK, fear, too.

I know this in such detail, because it's me. A long time ago. Monday, September 30th, 1974, to be precise. The papers are full of stuff about the upcoming election (another one!) The charts are full of glam rockers. But my mind is on other things. My first day at college.

Lucy – she's my younger sister – says that the Poly is 'crap', and that she's either going to Oxford University where she'll marry an aristocrat or to Chelsea College of Art where she'll take lots of drugs and become famous. Mother, on the other hand, is amazed that the Poly has accepted me at all: I wasn't exactly a shining light at school, was I?

They're even more unhelpful about the course I've chosen, Liberal Arts. Lucy says art should be illiberal, the prerogative of a brilliant elite. Mr Brown, a divorced (I'm not surprised) bank under-manager whom Mother sees far too often for my liking, says that studying such airy-fairy stuff is self-indulgent, especially given the current economic climate. Britain needs to pull its socks up and work harder, not sit around thinking about Liberal Arts.

Well, pooh to the lot of them. I'll be studying literature, music, art and – how about this? – philosophy. Philosophy, from the Greek *'philo'* which means 'love of' and *'sophos'* which means 'wisdom'. Plain, chubby, wilful-haired, not-exactly-a-shining-light-at-school Stella is about to become a Philosopher.

I give my beret a touch more tilt and push the strap of my shoulder-bag up a bit – it is thrillingly heavy with books – then march in. The platforms give me a series of pinches as I do so, but I ignore them. How many other young people, eager to escape ignorance, have walked through this arch over the years?

*

My first lecture!

I sit right at the front as I don't want to miss a single word. I set out my stuff. *Mon beret.* My Students' A4 Notepad, all 144 pages blank and waiting to be filled with wisdom (143 actually, as I have used one to put under the top sheet to stop the writing pressing through). My day-glo pink biro (a present from Lucy). My shiny new course textbook, *The Analytical Method, An Introduction to Logical Heuristics* by Dr Caradoc Peabody PhD (Cantab). The book is shiny because I haven't managed to get past page three, but never mind, the author is speaking to us in seven minutes' time – six, now – so all will soon become clear.

The room begins to fill. Nobody else sits right at the front.

Hmm. Nobody in our family has ever been to a place of Higher Education. Mother often says people shouldn't get 'ideas above their station', at which point Lucy always makes the same joke about does she mean Sydenham or Penge East. I've always disliked this notion. But is she right? Anyway, it's too late to change places, now.

An older lady – she must be at least 25 – is making her way down the row! She is wearing denims and a baggy, striped sweater covered in badges.

"Hi," she says, taking a seat one away from me. "I'm Anna."

"Oh, er, I'm Stella."

"Exciting, isn't it? The start of a journey!"

"Yes!" I exclaim, then don't know what to say next.

"Nice beret," she adds after a long pause.

"*Merci*," I reply.

Was that a touch pretentious?

Oui, I suddenly know, but luckily I'm saved from further embarrassment by the sound of footsteps on the podium.

I have been imagining what a Philosopher will look like. A beard. A leather jacket. A cigarette dangling from the corner of his mouth. Shades, which he will remove at some point to reveal penetrating, world-weary eyes.

Dr Caradoc Peabody PhD (Cantab) is wearing a tweed jacket, trousers made out of some kind of polyester, a bow tie and wire-rimmed glasses. He's clean-shaven, though it looks like he got a couple of nicks this morning.

'Oh, Stella, you can be so superficial!' I tell myself angrily. 'This man is a Philosopher. It his mind, his soul, not his choice in fabrics or his shaving skills, that you have come here to study.'

Dr Peabody strides to the lectern – well, he just walks, actually – places his notes on it and looks round the room. "Good morning, students," he says. A globule of spit lands on my Student's A4 Notepad. "What do you think this course is about?" Another globule lands, a couple of inches closer to me than the first one. I think it's the Ts that do it.

"Philosophy," says someone.

"Correct. Can we be a bit more specific? What is philosophy about?"

The globules are getting closer. This must be a test! I'd drown in spit to become a Philosopher.

"Wisdom," says a voice near me. Anna's. I suddenly want her to be my best friend, and regret lapsing into French all the more.

However, Dr Peabody doesn't seem impressed. "Wisdom?" he echoes back in a querulous tone.

"Right and wrong?" says another voice.

"Right and wrong?" The same tone. Clearly our answers are too obvious. Too shallow. Too – dare I say it? – *jejune.*

"The meaning of life?" says a third student.

Now that's got it, surely. But the Philosopher just frowns. My God, this is going to be so deep!

A silence falls, profound and existential. I imagine they have silences like this on the *Rive Gauche*, when Jean-Paul Sartre has raised a particularly baffling question about our place in the cosmos.

"What do all the answers you have given me have in common? Think, everybody, think!" (Ks have the spit-projecting effect too, though fortunately not quite as powerful.)

"They're words," says a male voice from the back.

I repress a giggle. Typical of the stupidest kind of boy – showing off; thinks he's funny when everyone else knows he's an idiot.

A grin creeps across Peabody's face. No doubt he's thought of some brilliant put-down.

"At last!" he says. "A philosophical answer. They are words. Which is what philosophy is about. Words. What do we mean when we use words? One of you said 'the meaning of life'. What did you mean by the word 'meaning'?" He stares at the unfortunate individual who made the suggestion.

"Well, er, what it's for," she stammers back.

"What's it's *for*," Peabody echoes, his grin expanding. "What do you mean by 'for'?"

"Er, dunno… What's the point of it all?"

"The *point* of it all?" says Peabody triumphantly. He extracts a pencil from his jacket pocket and jabs it into the least fleshless bit of his thumb. "What is the point of this pencil? It has a point, but what is the point of it? If I write with it sufficiently so that it becomes blunt, does it still have a point? Has it become a pointless pencil?"

Nobody replies.

"This troublesome ambiguity occurs because 'point' is a word. This is a point. You could say I am pointing at the point. But the word 'point' is not a point. Which is exactly my point."

He pauses, enjoying a victor's grin, then comes back to earth.

"In this series of lectures, I want to look at some of the ways we use – and abuse – words, and what philosophers have done to bring clarity – and, sadly, obscurity – to the proceedings. As I said in my book…"

*

"Bollocks!" says Anna as we sit down in the refectory with two Styrofoam cups of coffee.

"He's supposed to be the expert."

"Expert, my arse." Anna looks me full in the eye, daring me to contradict her. I feel a wave of reassurance.

But waves splatter onto beaches and turn to froth. *Sydenham or Penge East, Stella?*

"I don't think Dr Peabrain has the answers *we* are looking for," Anna continues.

"No," I reply, cresting a mighty new wave.

Anna takes a sip of coffee. "God, this stuff's revolting. Now, what's next? Ah. *Literature 101.* Should be more like it! Philosophy, the way they do it here, anyway, is just a lot of middle-aged men quibbling about words. Literature is about life. Love, ambition, loyalty, betrayal!"

I want to learn more about these things.

*

We get to the lecture theatre early, but don't sit right at the front in case Dr D Spiggott has the same spittle-control problem as Dr Peabody. The room fills. Time passes. Students begin whispering to one another. Anna starts packing her pens away and mutters about trying the Union bar – then a side door opens and a man in a T-shirt, scruffy jeans and a donkey jacket walks in. There's a bulb not working on the other side of the stage, and I assume he's come to fix it.

He stops at the lectern and turns to us.

"'Ello. I'm Dave Spiggott. 'Ow many of you actually enjoy 'literature'? Old novels, poetry, that sort of thing."

Anna puts her hand up at once. I follow her.

"I 'ate it," Dr D Spiggott continues. "We are in the middle of the ultimate crisis of late Capitalism, and what do I find on this reading list? Jane Austen: petty bourgeois tittle-tattle. DH Lawrence: fascist sympathizer and traitor to the working class. TS Eliot: the pseudo-mystical outpourings of an anti-Semitic bank clerk… Luckily for you, I have something more substantial." He produces a small red book and waves it at us. "The Thoughts of Chairman Mao Tse Tung!"

*

After lunch, we have *Introduction to Music* from a Dr S Licht. I say I'm not going, but Anna says give it a chance.

Our lecturer appears on time, which puts him ahead of Dr Spiggott, but he looks terribly old. As he shuffles across the stage, I begin to wonder if he'll make it to the lectern before he has an unpleasant accident and has to be wheeled off to Lewisham General.

Sydenham or Penge East, Stella?

He finally reaches his goal – phew! – and begins to speak. "Good afternoon, everybody." Actually, his voice is pretty robust. "I'm here to teach you the History of Music. In a series of ten lectures of an hour each. This is, of course, a completely impossible task."

Oh, God. Here we go again.

"The study of music is, at its deepest, an investigation into what it means to be human," he continues. "It is about what it means to live, what it means to feel joy, wonder, love and pain. It is also a study of history, of how events and cultures have moulded the human psyche in different ways. It is a study of theology, of our relationship to the divine. It is a

7

study of psychology: what manner of creature are we, that we can create and love great music? It is, perhaps most of all, a study of philosophy, of the great moral and directional questions of human life… So ten one-hour lectures are hardly going to be enough. But I shall do my best."

I turn to Anna, who turns to me at exactly the same time with exactly the same look of triumph.

*

Next day, I'm walking from the library to the refectory, when I see Dr Licht ahead of me. I am overcome by my usual shyness, but I make myself run and catch him up.

"My friend and I really liked your lecture," I say.

"Oh. Thank you."

"It's full of – gosh, I don't know how to say this – interesting thoughts about the meaning of life and art and philosophy and all that sort of thing."

"You're most kind."

I feel emboldened. "I don't really understand our actual philosophy course."

He nods. "But you are interested in the subject?"

"Yes. Very much."

"Good," he says, then falls silent. And actually, that is the end of the conversation, apart from a polite 'goodbye', as after the next swing doors (the Poly is full of swing doors) we have to go in different directions.

*

Joe is sitting in his corner with his usual extra-strong tea. *Ballroom Blitz* by The Sweet (or is it just Sweet? Who cares?) is playing on the radio.

"So how's it going?" asks Carlo.

"OK," I reply hesitantly.

Carlo's Café is my second home. I waitressed here for a year before starting my academic adventure.

Carlo frowns. "OK? Is that all?"

"Yes…" I reply.

Dr Licht's lecture was amazing, but as I watched him shuffle away after those swing doors, I felt that was my future shuffling away with him. *Stella is a bit of a dreamer*, my reports used to say. *Stella lacks the aptitude for proper study.* I just hope the old boy forgets the conversation ever occurred.

"Life should be more than 'OK', Stella," says Carlo. "It should be amazing. You'll always be welcome back here if being a student just stays 'OK'. We had fun!"

"That's… very kind," I reply.

We did, too, but I always felt I wanted more. But was 'more' a delusion? Green grass on the other side of a fence, which turned out to be plastic? Perhaps I should take Carlo up on his offer.

Sweet (The Sweet?) fade out on a guitar solo, and are replaced by a live studio debate on platform heels. Have they become too high? No way, says Trisha from Greenford.

Give it a *few* more days…

I light a *Gauloise* and start coughing.

*

Dr Licht's next lecture is about mediaeval music – and mediaeval theology, history, painting and literature, the life of Hildegard of Bingen and an analogy between the Holy Roman Empire and the debate about whether Britain should remain in the Common Market, which it joined last year, much to Mother's disgust (Mr Brown disagreed, saying it would be good for business). I look up at the clock, and see with heartbreak that it is time to finish.

"Before I go – I have been asked by one of you – I can't see you – Oh, yes, there you are – to say more about philosophy and its relationship to music. Sadly, there is not time for me to do this properly, and you already have an excellent Introduction to Philosophy course. However, I do not wish to disappoint the young lady, or anyone else with a similar curiosity: I would be happy to give some informal seminars on the subject for the rest of this term. If anyone is interested, I shall be in my office at 6.30 tomorrow evening."

Belonging

I turn up early just in case there's a crowd, but actually I'm the first and it only ends up with six of us. Me, Anna, a couple of other girls about whom I now remember nothing (sorry, ladies, if you're reading this now), and two males: a rather sad-looking older man – like Anna, way into his twenties – whom Anna immediately nicknames Big Ears for obvious reasons, and a mousy lad in a purple shirt and flared trousers, who inevitably ends up as Noddy.

Maybe it's just as well we are so few, as Dr Licht's office isn't very big. It's also very full, with a piano, a violin, music stands, scores, loose sheets of music paper, a bust labelled 'Wolfgang Amadeus Mozart', boxes of tape, an old reel-to-reel tape recorder with Bakelite buttons, a pair of loudspeakers with torn fronts, and, most of all, books. There are books on music, books on philosophy, books on history, books on psychology, books on religion, books on sociology, books on art, books full of poetry, books I haven't a clue what they're about. There's a complete Shakespeare, six volumes of Gibbon's *Decline and Fall of the Roman Empire*, half a shelf of European novels I've heard of but know shamefully little about: *Madame Bovary, Anna Karenina, Crime and Punishment.* There are books piled in corners. Dr Licht's desk-lamp sits on four books about mediaeval history. There are books under the tape-recorder, books under Anna's seat, books behind the door. The place even smells of books, which might seem musty and boring to some people but which to me is intoxicating.

The Doctor glances at his watch and asks Anna to close

the door.

"Welcome to what I'm going to call my Enlightenment Club," he begins once she is back in her seat. "I'm afraid I was dishonest when I spoke to the class as a whole. I do *not* consider the lectures given by the Philosophy Department 'excellent' at all. I consider them to have betrayed both the great thinkers of the past and – even more seriously – the curious young minds of the future."

He looks round at us proudly. "Philosophy is a quest, not a word game. It's a quest that began when one of our distant ancestors looked around and began to wonder. What? When? How? Why? The last, above all: why? The quest is still continuing. It has no end, really – it will last as long as there are human beings on this earth."

My beret is in my bag, and I give it a little squeeze.

"In these sessions we can only eavesdrop on a tiny part of this, the great human adventure," Dr Licht goes on. "Apologies to any Hellenophiles, Senecans, mediaevalists or anyone interested in the world's many other great intellectual traditions: Hinduism, Islam, Buddhism, Confucianism. Time compels me to start in Europe, at the dawning of what we call the modern age. In 1619, a young Frenchman is sitting by a stove on a winter day, lost in puzzlement. He wants to know what to dedicate himself to. Science? Religion? Are these compatible? More deeply, he wonders how he could *know* if they were? What does it mean when he says he 'knows' something? He is not just picking over the minutiae of language; he wants to engage with life with the full force of his intelligence. In other words, he is a true philosopher."

'Like us,' I think. The six of us, who have made the effort to step out of the run of things and come here to learn…

"The generation of thinkers before our young *penseur* had been particularly troubled by the last of his questions," the Doctor continues. "How do you know when you know something? For them, true knowledge was impossible; in the end, you either relied on faith or you faced the philosopher's nightmare – nihilism. Nihilism means that nothing that we or anyone else can assert or believe has any absolute, guaranteed validity or meaning. Anyone who has *truly* experienced this state of mind will tell you it is terrifying."

He pauses to let this sink in, then recommences. "Our young man – his name is René Descartes by the way – does *not* want to end up with nihilism. But he won't accept easy answers. He will doubt everything he can, and see if there is anything left. Anything at all. If there isn't, he will accept nihilism with all its anguish."

Dr Licht takes us on Descartes' journey of doubt. Can we trust our senses? No, we misidentify things all the time. So what about abstract, logical structures? In mathematics, things can be proven – but what is proof? Maybe there's a demon, trying to fool us into believing something to be 'proven' that is actually false. Can we even prove we exist? Maybe this demon is fooling us about this, too.

I give myself a reassuring pinch. I exist.

But supposing a demon is making me think I've just felt a pinch?

The thought is scary. Perhaps I'm not cut out for this philosophy stuff after all…

"Of course, Descartes did find an answer," the Doctor continues, "or we wouldn't be talking about him now. Does anyone know what it was?"

"*Cogito ergo sum,*" pipes up a familiar voice.

13

"Thank you, Anna. *Cogito ergo sum*. I think, therefore I am. You can doubt the truth of any thought, but you can't deny there's thinking going on. So something must be doing the thinking. So I, as the thinker, must exist. Clever, eh?"

Of course I can be a Philosopher! Demons – what a ridiculous idea!

"Having established a point of certainty," Dr Licht goes on, "Descartes went on to build a system on it, one that both explained the world – or at least provided the tools to explain it – and generated a moral code by which to run his life. How well he did this, we shall consider next week, but for now I want you just to ponder his basic method. *Find one point of absolute certainty, then build on it.* That, ladies and gentlemen, is the basic technique of philosophy. It has nothing to do with playing around with words."

He lets us digest that thought for a moment, then reaches across to the tape recorder.

"You may be wondering if it has anything to do with music. An excellent question and a true philosopher's one. It is one that I shall answer... another time. Right now, let's just listen to some."

He pushes a button. The reels creak; the speakers hiss.

"Ladies and gentlemen," says the Doctor, "I present to you the *Requiem* of Wolfgang Amadeus Mozart."

*

"Hi Stella," says Carlo. "You look happy."

"I am."

"Great!" He pauses. "Don't tell me! You've fallen in love!"

"In a way." I remove *le beret* and place it proudly in front of me. Carlo looks puzzled, then asks if I want my usual milky coffee.

"Yes, please. That's one thing the Poly can't do!"

He disappears behind the espresso machine. "So, tell me," he says over the hisses and gurgles.

"It's this group. We talk about such interesting things. We listen to wonderful music. Mozart's *Requiem*. Ever heard it?"

"That sort of stuff never did much for me."

Y Viva Espana comes on the radio.

"You should. It's… amazing," I tell him. "This guy is teaching us all about art and music and philosophy and…" I'm lost for words for a moment. "He turned on this old tape recorder, and this music began playing. It was sad, incredibly sad, but happy in its own way too. That doesn't make sense, does it, but that's how it was… Then voices joined in, all singing across each other but fitting together perfectly. Then just a solo female, so lovely and pure. More voices. Then it went all quiet. Then they began swirling round and round and round, and grew and grew till they came to this incredible climax. It turned me inside out. It was so beautiful."

"An incredible climax sounds good," says Carlo from behind the machine.

I ignore this. "I'm a Philosopher, now," I say.

"Ah. What is your philosophy?"

"I haven't got one yet. Philosophy is a way of looking at things. A method. Find one point of absolute certainty – a Cartesian point, we call it, after René Descartes – and build on it."

"Ah." Carlo brings the coffee. It feels odd being waited on by my former boss, but he seems happy enough. Not that anything ever seems to get him down (Why can't I be like that?) (Maybe I can, now!)

"Descartes went on this journey of doubt," I continue. "He refused to accept anything that could be doubted. Anything – sense impressions, mathematics, logic – even the fact that he existed."

"Sounds a bit of a nutter to me."

"No, well, he came up with this formula, something he couldn't doubt. A point of certainty. *Cogito ergo sum.* I think, therefore I am."

He looks puzzled. "You are what?"

"Just 'I am'. I think therefore I am."

"Oh."

Silence falls, apart from Sylvia off on her hols to Spain, another gurgle from the machine and two cars hooting at each other on the South Circular Road outside.

"It suits you, Stella."

"What?"

"Mozart's incredible climax. All that thinking therefore you are, even if you don't seem to be anything in particular. All that brainy stuff."

"They said I was stupid at school."

"I never thought that, Stella. Ever. They were the stupid ones."

*

By the end of the Club's next session, Descartes' attempt to build systematic thought on his *cogito* are in tatters.

OK, thinking is going on, but what else can you deduce from that? *I* think, but what is this 'I'? A discrete individual or a deluded part of something bigger?

Never mind, the Doctor insists, that's an interesting question. What is this 'I'? And most important of all, is his method. *Find one point of absolute certainty, then build on it.*

Instead, we look at the work of Descartes' great rival, the British 'empiricist', John Locke. Locke had a point of certainty, too, and a much simpler one than Descartes' maxim. Truth comes to us though our senses.

"Simple!" says the Doctor, tapping the tape recorder with a biro. "That noise was real; the pen is real, the tape recorder is real. OK, our senses can mislead us sometimes, but over time the errors cancel out. We can use what we sense to build a tried and tested picture of objective reality that we can really trust."

I spend the next week wondering what all the philosophical fuss is about – but at the next session the Doctor introduces a Scotsman, David Hume, who points out that our senses tell us nothing beyond the moment.

The Doctor does the tap again. "All we actually *know* – at the moment of experience only – is that some event is happening in our brain." Another tap. "Tapping noise, then. Everything else…" He gives a big shrug. "Do things cause other things? Maybe. Or maybe the world is just one big jumble of coincidences. We don't *know*. And as for right versus wrong, or ugliness versus beauty – these are just emotional reactions, with no objective value or meaning. If you like the sound of chalk on a blackboard and I like Mozart's *Requiem*, that's just how we are, and there is nothing more to be said."

"Isn't that nihilism?" Anna asks.

"Yes. But Hume didn't mind. His advice was to go for a nice long walk, forget about it and get on with day-to-day life. Of course, I can't accept that answer."

"So what do we do?"

"We keep asking questions. Let's listen to some more music!"

*

The week races by. Then we meet Karl Marx. He suggested that ultimate truth was found in history, more specifically in the struggle between the classes. Class power spreads itself into all areas of life, not just how we work and earn, but how we think, know and feel.

At Dr Spiggott's next lecture, I sit in the front row and mutter 'right on' at regular intervals – but at the next Club meeting, Dr Licht says that history actually shows Marx to be fatally flawed. He made loads of predictions, virtually none of which have come true. But if you point that out to Marxists, they will tell you that you are suffering from false consciousness. Marx's system has its own inbuilt logic that makes it impossible to criticize. You are either a True Believer or an outsider.

"This puts Marxism on a par with the delusions of cult leaders," the Doctor continues. "So we have to look elsewhere for our Cartesian point of certainty. Next week, we'll start looking inside ourselves."

We do that courtesy of Sigmund Freud. His Cartesian point was sexual desire and the damage caused by our attempts to repress it. That Friday, I go to the Liberal Society disco and come on really strong to a nice-looking young man called Peter. Unfortunately for my *id*, he drinks too much and passes out before it can achieve gratification ('Serves you right,' says my *superego*.) And, of course, next week the Doctor says that I was wasting my time, philosophically anyway (and emotionally: I pass Peter in the corridor a few days later and he looks straight through me). Like Marx, Freud created a model that repelled critical analysis: if you disagree with him, you are repressing the truth. You need, not ten years in a Gulag, which is the reward for disbelief in actual Marxist states, but more therapy.

"Freudianism's just another cult, I'm afraid," he says with a smile. "Let's go in the opposite direction, and look at science."

This isn't anyone's philosophy, but a method that has just evolved. And look at all the amazing things it has produced! Anna says something about the Atom Bomb, but she cooked me a lovely dinner the other evening and used an electric stove, not two sticks rubbed together over a pile of twigs.

Then the Doctor reads us some 19th century material about racial types and how some are 'superior' to others, and how this was 'proven' by the 'sciences' of the time: craniometry and anthropometrics. He follows this with a description of the long-running attempts by tobacco companies to prove smoking and cancer are unrelated. Science, he says, spends a lot of time telling people what they want to, expect to, or have paid to hear.

It's nearly the end of term, now. Are we going to end up nihilists after all?

The sessions always conclude with music – Bach, Beethoven, but most beloved of all, Mozart. The *Requiem*, he says, 'has everything', so we listen to that a lot. Sometimes we also look at books of great paintings or read poetry (the Doctor particularly likes the English Romantics: Keats, Coleridge, Wordsworth…) These things always seem to offer consolation for the scrabbling attempts by philosophers to make absolute sense of things.

"You are becoming Philosophers and Lovers of Great

Art," the Doctor tells us.

The rest of my time at the Poly seems pointless in comparison. Lectures, apart from Introduction to Music, are chores that I sit through. My essays are late and poor. But I don't care. Once a week, I am finding Enlightenment.

*

A few vaguely Christmassy things appear around the Poly in early December, but as a Philosopher and Lover of Great Art, I consider myself above such fripperies. The penultimate session of the Enlightenment Club is coming up, on which the Doctor has promised to reveal the route that he believes leads to philosophical truth.

The night before it, I can't sleep. I have philosophy whirring round in my head – 'first cause', 'deduction', '*it must be the case that*…', 'Cartesian point'. I see the Philosophers – all men, Anna points out, but if they can take away the pain that I feel, of not knowing and of needing to know, then I don't care what sex they are.

I oversleep and miss 'Modernism in Art and Design' – but I don't care. The whole day is a blur, but finally it is six fifteen and I can't be anywhere else but waiting in the corridor outside Dr Licht's office.

He lets me in early, and invites me to take something to read: I pick at random and spend a quarter of an hour learning about how, at the time of the Black Death, people walked through the streets of Europe's cities whipping each other in the hope that, by driving out their own sin, they would persuade God to stop the plague. Were people really that crazy?

The Doctor waits till we have all arrived – Big Ears is late – and then holds up a book with a picture on the cover of a man with a ridiculous walrus moustache.

"Friedrich Nietzsche," he says proudly, making me give myself another talking-to for judging by appearances. "This man gets blamed for all sorts of things, including the rise of the Nazis. This is, of course, a calumny, as his sister outlived him and doctored his work after his death."

"I, by contrast, place him next to Descartes," the Doctor goes on. "Like Descartes, he was prepared to challenge all conventional certainties. Like Descartes, he ended up looking inside himself for ultimate truth – *I* think, *I* am. But Nietzsche went deeper. For him, truth was not a thing to be found but an active principle, seeking expression. It was life itself. We are drawn to it – he talked about a 'will to power', and stupid people thought he meant political power, but of course he meant the inner power that comes from living truthfully.

"That truth is subtly different in every individual human being. Nietzsche wrote: *In their heart, everyone knows well enough that they are a unique being, only once on this earth, and by no extraordinary chance will such a marvellously picturesque piece of diversity in unity as this ever be put together a second time.* That's you, Anna. And you, Stella. And you, Eustace – "

He carries on round the room, but my attention is no longer there but inside, contemplating a unique being, only once on this earth, called Stella Tranter. The thought is shocking and freeing. I am not just the shy suburban nobody people take me for. *I am a unique being, only once on this earth.*

Yes!!!

"So there we have it," the Doctor is saying. "Your Cartesian point is within you. You have to find it, as does everybody born to live on this earth. You can't look in the same place as other people, as there is only one you, and only one deepest inner truth, which you must seek out and then live by. 'To thine own self be true,' as Shakespeare said."

Anna is nodding enthusiastically. One of the girls is scribbling in a notebook. Big Ears is frowning.

"At the beginning of our sessions," says the Doctor, "I asked what this had to do with music, and I promised I'd answer. Now I shall. Friedrich Nietzsche was also a musician and composer, though not a very good one. Luckily for us he was an outstanding listener. He realized that a point of unshakeable, inner truth can be aesthetic, not logical or even expressible in words. It can be the experience of a moment of absolute, transcendent beauty."

A look of deep contentment steals across the Doctor's face. "That's how it was for me. I remember listening to the *Requiem* as a young man, and suddenly knowing that I had found something that I could build my life around. Something solid, something absolute, a glowing source of inner power that would never let me down. To me, this knowledge overcame all the arguments that bedevil the philosophies we have looked at this term – all except for Nietzsche's, of course." He pauses. "Let's listen to Wolfgang Amadeus Mozart. My truth, my Cartesian point of absolute certainty."

The speakers hiss. The first, lilting bars of the *Requiem* fill the tiny room. The voices begin to swell. Then he turns the volume down.

"Of course, that was *my* experience," he says. "What will yours be?"

Big Ears starts to speak, but the Doctor holds up a hand.

"Don't say anything now. This is just the beginning. Come and see me in twenty years' time and tell me what you have found."

He fades the music back in.

*

In our last gathering we listen to music, look at more art and read extracts from some other Philosophers: Jean-Paul Sartre, GE Moore, more from Nietzsche. *Life without music would be a mistake.*

As I sit and soak in their wisdom, I am on the edge of tears I am so happy. Sydenham or Penge East? No, *my* station is Berlin, Hauptbahnhof. Paris, St-Germain-des-Près. Florence, whatever the railway station in Florence is called.

At the end, Anna gets to her feet and holds out a bottle of Champagne (she organized a whip-round after the last class: everyone contributed fulsomely except Big Ears, who only had 13p on him and promised to pay his part today but has now forgotten his wallet). "You've been brilliant, Stanislas," she says.

"So have you all," the Doctor replies. His eyes begin to glisten. "We could continue next term, if you wish. I'll find some time – I've a busy schedule, but where there's a will… There are many fine works of Great Art we could consider and puzzling philosophical questions we could investigate. If that would be of interest to you, of course."

"Yes, please!" we reply, virtually in unison.

*

Christmas that year is special, after all. I ask for (and get) books as presents. Nietzsche's *The Birth of Tragedy from the Spirit of Music*. Moore's *Principia Ethica* (rather hard going). *La Nausée* by Jean-Paul Sartre (even harder going: I'd wanted it in English). A book on anarchism from Lucy.

On New Year's Eve she goes to a 'happening' at someone called Sebastian's. I'm secretly hoping Anna will

23

invite me over, but she's recently got involved with one of the sociology lecturers and he has invited her to a party in Greenwich. Actually, I don't mind. I have my books and I have my music. Great Art.

Mother retires early, muttering something about being another year older. "You see the New Year in for me, Stella. You're the one with the future."

I sit on the sofa and read a little of *The Birth of Tragedy*, then listen to my present to myself, a brand new recording of the *Requiem*. Our spindly-legged Radiogram with the Formica top that doesn't fit properly has never sounded so majestic! I get so lost in the glory of Wolfgang Amadeus Mozart that I forget to look at the clock. Suddenly it's 12.07 and 1975.

I open Anna's present to me, a bottle of dark red wine. I pour myself a glass, sniff its heady aroma and drink a toast to the Enlightened future that will now be mine.

Rebelling

Notice to all students on the Liberal Arts course. Please note that this term's lectures for Introduction to Music will be given by Professor Tyrwhitt.

The note is in my pigeonhole on the first day of the new term. Is Dr Licht OK?

Anna isn't in her usual place in the library or her usual corner in the bar. I queue for the telephone – there's a bank of five, but the coin boxes of four of them are out of order: my fellow students have been putting ring-pulls from cans into the slots designed for 2p pieces. When I finally get to the front of the queue and call her, there's no answer.

Only one thing for it. Through a couple of swing doors, up a staircase, along a gloomy corridor with peeling paint and frayed carpet. *Department of Music.* But Dr Licht's office is locked. No note on the door.

From a room marked *Departmental Secretary* comes the clatter of a typewriter. I'm nervous about interrupting adults at work (I know, technically I am one, but I don't feel adult in a way that people with jobs, families all that stuff must do). But I have to find out.

The Departmental Secretary is one of these immaculately neat women: cherry lipstick, bobbed hair that is as crisp as candyfloss. She turns heavily made-up eyes on me as I put my head round the door. "Can I help?"

"Yes. I… Dr Licht… Is he OK?"

"He's fine. But he's taking a sabbatical this term."

"A what?"

"A break."

"From everything?"

"From everything."

"Oh."

"Are you on the 101 course?"

"Yes."

"Professor Tyrwhitt is taking it. You should have had a note in your pigeonhole." The perfect lips break for a second into a grin: *now* will you go away.

I carry on. "I thought Dr Licht was a brilliant lecturer, and I'm really going to miss him."

"I'll tell him that. What's your name?"

"Stella. Stella Tranter. I'm… one of his philosophy students."

Suddenly the cherry lips tremble and the candyfloss looks about to disintegrate. "You lot! If you knew how much trouble you've caused!"

"Trouble?"

"With the Philosophy Department. I had that man who spits in here, raving. He said it was their job to teach philosophy; who did we think we were? As if it were *my* fault!"

"They told Stanislas he had to stop his group," the woman goes on. "He refused. So the Dean was bought in, and Stanislas still refused. Then half the Philosophy Department threatened to resign. Good riddance, in my view, but it was too much for Stanislas and he gave in. He's now taking a term's leave of absence, and the rest of us are up to our elbows in work. It's been a nightmare."

Then she stops. The lips and the hair become solid again. "Now, if you'd kindly leave, I have a lot of work to do."

I nod sympathetically. "You don't have his home number, do you?"

"No, I do not."

It's a lie, I'm sure, but I don't feel up to challenging her.

*

Maybe Anna will be in the refectory. But she isn't. I get myself a bowl of chicken soup, then spot Big Ears. I feel a sudden need to be with him. He may not have been the most interactive member of the Club, but he's still one of us. A fellow voyager into truth and meaning. I go and sit opposite him, stirring the soup to cool it down a bit and feeling rather bad about the nickname, even if Anna and I just used it to each other.

"Isn't it awful?" I say.

"What?"

"About Stanislas."

He shrugs.

"You don't care?" I ask, horrified.

"Life has to go on."

His ears start to redden and suddenly I know, as surely as Descartes knew he thought therefore he was, that…

"You told them, didn't you?"

"No," he replies and looks away. His ears are ablaze.

"You did!"

"OK, I happened to mention the matter."

"To Peabrain?"

"Doctor Pea*body* and I were having our end-of-term tutorial. I started talking about Nietzsche. He asked me where I'd learnt so much about this individual, so I told him."

"Why?"

"Because I was asked," he snaps back. "Dr Peabody says that irrationalist philosophers are intellectually irresponsible and can do a lot of damage. He says that those meetings were very unhealthy."

"Well, don't go to them, then, you bloody little sneak!"

Big Ears scowls at me. "You're getting hysterical, Stella."

I'm not quite sure what happens next.

No. I am totally sure what happens next. I get to my feet, pick up my soup bowl and empty it over his head.

He sits there, immobilized with shock. I don't move either, just stand watching Polytechnic of the South Circular Student Union chicken soup oozing down his forehead.

"Sorry…" I say.

A drip forms on the end of his nose, getting bigger and bigger then falls with a plop onto the table. I reach for a serviette, but there isn't one.

"Terribly sorry…"

I turn and run.

*

We (Anna, me and Noddy) form the Enlightenment Club Action Committee, or ECAC. The Committee has its first Meeting in the Union Bar the next day. I have a vodka beforehand to get in the mood.

The meeting goes well. We produce a slogan: *Reinstate The South Circular Poly One!* I get another vodka, and suggest we boycott Peabrain's lectures. And how about a protest march? We'll need posters, too. A clenched fist? A raised Kalashnikov?

"We'd better go and see Stanislas first," says Anna, "Ask him what he wants us to do. We don't want him losing his job."

I order a third vodka, but she's right, of course.

Anna looks the Doctor up in the phone book and rings him. He invites us round to tea. We hold a second meeting of

ECAC. Our decision to accept the offer of tea is unanimous.

*

I don't remember much about our journey, except that we take a 197 bus. And that the door of the Doctor's little terraced house is blue. He welcomes us in with a smile, invites us to sink into some old chairs, and disappears into a kitchen. In the background, a record is playing. Bach, it has to be Bach. He reappears with mugs of tea and ginger biscuits.

"Lovely music," I say.

He nods. "Scarlatti."

Anna takes her tea. "We're furious about what's happened."

He sighs. "I'm sorry."

"You don't have to be sorry!"

"I should have played the game better. I know academic politics."

"Fascists!" says Anna.

"No, Anna, they're pompous, bullying, hypocritical and blinkered, but they're not fascists. As a young man, I watched stormtroopers marching through the streets of Vienna. A few weeks later, Jewish friends of our family began to disappear. That's fascism, not a few ageing, second-rate academics defending their territory."

He falls silent. As do we, except for the sound of Noddy crunching on a biscuit. Then I have a bright idea. "Perhaps we could carry on our classes outside the Poly."

The Doctor shakes his head. "I had to give an undertaking not to teach any philosophy. I'm sorry, but that was part of the deal. It's not exactly easy to get jobs at my age. You are all quite right to look down on that 'saving for retirement' stuff – but the nearer retirement gets…"

Anna nods sympathetically.

"It's terribly kind of you to come here," he continues. "I really appreciate it. But I believe I have already given you the keys to being Philosophers and Lovers of Great Art."

"Find your Cartesian point!" says Anna.

"To thine own self be true!" I add.

Noddy helps himself to another biscuit.

*

I want to boycott Peabrain's lectures, but Stanislas says we ought to attend, otherwise we'll fail our exams, and what would be the point of that? At a third meeting of ECAC, it is decided by a vote of 2 (them) to 1 (me) to attend, but to sit at the back and take as few notes as possible.

The resolution is followed, but the day-glo pink biro makes no notes at all.

"That will be all," says Peabrain, squaring off his papers at the end of the lecture. Then he adds, "You'll be pleased to know, by the way, that I won't be organizing any extra-curricular musical appreciation classes."

I *can't* let that go by. I just can't.

*

The drab little office is, by Dr Licht's standards, bookless. Facing me are three people: a lecturer from some department I don't catch the name of; Dr Spiggott, apparently representing some Union or other; and the Dean of Studies.

"What was it you called Dr Peabody?" asks the Dean. "In a room full of students? At the top of your voice?"

I tell them.

"Aren't you ashamed?"

I was being true to myself: Peabody *is* a pompous, bullying, blinkered old hypocrite. But suddenly I feel guilt, not

30

pride.

"Y – yes," I reply.

"And then there's that business with Mr Crabbe and the soup," she continues. "You must, surely, have some remorse about that."

"Y – yes…"

"When we admitted you to the Polytechnic, Miss Tranter, we assumed a degree of responsible behaviour. A little youthful excess is always acceptable, but there are standards of civilized debate."

I'm trying to formulate some reply involving freedom of speech, but Dr Spiggott cuts in.

"I disagree. Mzz Tranter" (he speaks my appellation like an angry bee) "has a genuinely revolutionary consciousness. Anyone can sit around and have 'civilized debates'. What this Polytechnic, and this world, needs are people who take action." He grins at me. I smile weakly back.

"Like pouring soup over a fellow-student?" says the Dean.

"He was clearly a reactionary."

"And heckling a respected member of staff?" says the mystery lecturer.

"He's a reactionary, too."

The Dean sighs. "Hmm. Are you saying we should re-admit her, David?"

"Dave. Well, some sort of compromise. Start again next year. We're redesigning the course, anyway. More focus on developing a truly proletarian consciousness. Mzz Tranter is exactly the sort of student we need."

"Hmm. We've persuaded Mr Crabbe to drop the assault charges, but he may have objections to *Miss* Tranter's returning. And Dr Peabody has strong views on the bounds of academic debate." She turns to me. "Then there's the matter of your coursework, Miss Tranter. You seem to have very little interest in Liberal Arts." She sighs again. "Do you have *anything* to say for yourself?"

I try, but no words come out.

"Wise," says Dr Spiggott. "Philosophers only interpret the world," he adds, giving me a knowing wink. "*Our* job is to change it."

"Hmm," the Dean says again.

*

My expulsion letter arrives a couple of days later. There is nothing about starting again next year, either.

Lucy thinks I'm ultra-cool – for a few days, anyway. Mr Brown's daughter Jacqui walks straight past me on Dartmouth Road. No loss, but I'd rather snub her than be snubbed by the stuck-up little cow. Mother seems rather happy, telling me to 'look on the bright side' and that it's time for me to get a proper job. That Liberal Arts stuff wasn't for people who want to get on with real life, was it?

*

It's a month later. I phone Anna. We can still be friends, I'm sure. We chat about people at the Poly.

"How's Henry?" I ask.

"OK. It didn't really work out."

"Sorry to hear that."

"It was just a fling. I'm fine. What are you doing?"

"Er, I've signed up for another college."

"Good for you. Which one?"

"Oh, it's just a small one."

"What's it called?"

"Upper Norwood."

"Ah. I didn't know there was one there. Is that part of London University? I hope they have a better philosophy department."

"Upper Norwood is more, er, vocational."

"Vocational?"

"It's… a secretarial college."

"Oh."

Silence.

"It's not just typing," I say. "I'm going to do bookkeeping, sales, principles of marketing – all sorts of stuff."

"Oh."

"I have to earn a living."

"Yes." She sighs. "Dragsville, isn't it?" Another pause. "Well, I hope I'll see you around some time."

"Of course!"

Silence.

"Look, it's good to hear from you, Stella. I've got to go now. Good luck!"

"Thanks. Bye."

"Bye."

She puts the phone down; I sit with it for a while listening first to the silence and then the whistling noise that follows.

Interlude 1

"We did 'how to read a balance sheet' today," I say.

"Interesting," says Mother. "How do you read a balance sheet?"

I start explaining about assets and liabilities but get confused about where debtors and creditors go.

"Interesting," Mother says again.

"We're doing more tomorrow," I add.

Constable's *Hay Wain* looks down on us from above the fireplace. Opposite it, Grandpa Scowcroft smiles cheerily beneath the military cap that he was wearing on 1st July 1916 when he was blown to pieces. Another grandfather, Uncle Horace's clock, tocks in the hall. There's a smell of cabbage.

Lucy is now at college studying Art, Music and Drama. She goes upstairs as soon as she can, and starts listening to her new music. It's called 'punk', and is played by Americans with ridiculous names like Iggy Pop.

"What a horrible row," says Mother.

I smile, enjoying the fact that we actually agree about something. "Why don't we listen to some music, too?"

"That would be nice, Stella. But not that *Requiem* thing of yours. I find it rather morbid. How about something a bit gentler?" She starts looking through her own collection. "*Manuel and his Music of the Mountains*. Nice and relaxing."

Philosophy, Great Art and the City: Punk

I graduate from Upper Norwood in summer 1976 with a Distinction in accounts, which I discover, once I've got the debtors and creditors thing sorted out, that I'm rather good at. Unlike the confusing business of dealing with people, there are right and wrong answers. Figures belong in particular columns, and have to add up. If something isn't working, there is a reason, which one can find out and then do something about.

I start applying for jobs. At my first interview, I tell a balding man with a bright orange tie about my Distinction. He doesn't seem hugely impressed.

I know; he wants to look deeper.

"At the Poly, I was a member of a group called The Enlightenment Club," I say proudly. "We made a serious study of Philosophy. Descartes, Locke, Hume," (better leave out Marx) "Freud and Nietzsche."

He scratches his head and a gentle snowfall of dandruff floats down onto his shoulders. "We don't need philosophers at Amalgamated Iron, Miss Tranter. We need people who'll roll their sleeves up and get on with it."

"We studied Great Art, too," I add, but he just scratches his head again, creating a second snowfall.

"We'll let you know," he says.

I stop mentioning Philosophy or Great Art at interviews, and soon get offered a secretarial job at a City solicitors' practice.

After a few months, I find a flat. My base, for my new life in the Big City. I shall not give up my passion. I shall be a Philosopher and Lover of Great Art in my spare time. London, surely, is *the* place to do this.

I decorate the flat myself – Lucy, bless her, comes and helps, even though I reject all her suggestions. I do not want a bedroom painted all black. And why would I want a huge mirror on the ceiling, even if I could afford it?

I buy some pictures: old posters for concerts or Royal Academy Summer Exhibitions, and some reproduction portraits: Wolfgang Amadeus; Élisabeth-Louise Vigée Le Brun, smiling and intelligent-eyed in a gorgeous plumed straw hat; Anne, Countess of Chesterfield, by Gainsborough, so pensive in her flowing blue dress.

Meanwhile, Lucy's 'music' becomes all the rage. She joins a band and moves into a squat in Islington.

I have some special cards made, with pictures of a book and a treble clef on.

Stella Tranter
Flat 6
32 Eaglescliffe Road
LONDON W12

Lucy doesn't have any cards made.

One evening, I'm sitting in 32 Eaglescliffe re-reading Eduard Möricke's *Mozart's Journey to Prague*, happily immersed in a bygone era of artifice and elegance (OK, and patronizing ways of addressing females, but Constanze knows how to stand up for herself, as I'm sure she did in real life). It's a short story about the couple travelling from Vienna to Prague, a weeks' journey in those days, and descending, by a series of chances, on a family for an evening *en route*, delighting them, before moving on. Beautiful but sad, too, as we know Wolfgang Amadeus has not long to live. (Fate, why did you do that to us all?)

I sit back and imagine a knock on the door. It's Mozart and Constanze, on a journey from Acton to Notting Hill, wanting to pop for a bit (in my fantasy, of course, they speak English. Or I speak German. What does it matter?) I make them some dinner. I thank him, maybe a little overeffusively, for his music. He accepts my compliments with a kindly smile, and tells me what it's like to be a Great Artist. Then they have to be off… Max, the serious, competent, sensitive young man who is one of the party in Möricke's story, is with us too. He is in less of a hurry to leave. Instead, he turns bashful, then looks into my eyes…

The phone rings. It's not Mozart, Constanze or Max, but Lucy. Do I fancy coming to a gig?

"I'm busy," I tell her brusquely.

She says there's an A and R man from some record company coming and they need as many people there as possible and –

"Sorry, Lucy," I cut in. "I really am tired."

"Selling your soul."

"Earning a living," I say. I restrain myself from adding 'Subsidizing you'; Lucy is on the dole.

Back to my book. But I feel bad, not about my refusal – why should I subject myself to that racket? – but about my tone. Next day, I ring her and ask how it went.

"The bastard didn't turn up."

"Oh. I'm sorry to hear that." I do mean that. Not just because of any guilt about my reactions last night, but because

I really don't want her to fail. I love her; if she became a pop star I'd be delighted for her.

"We're playing the Greyhound next Tuesday if you fancy coming along. It's just down the road from you."

"Maybe," I say.

*

I expect everyone to stare at Lucy as we board the bus at Shepherd's Bush, with her Mohican, nose-stud, micro-skirt and torn stockings. But everyone seems to look at *me*.

Well, she rang up again, and sounded like she really *needed* me to come. I'll only do it once.

We get off half way down Fulham Palace Road and walk to a shabby-looking pub with torn posters outside. Tonight it's *Anne T Social and the Fuckwits*. Soon after, a dented white van pulls up and a tall, rather striking man gets out. Lucy introduces him as Jeff, 'our guitarist'. I'm not sure how a Philosopher and Lover of Great Art should greet the guitarist of the Fuckwits, so grin and say "Hi".

"Delighted," he replies, making a kind of bow. I wonder if that was genuine or taking the mickey. The latter, probably.

"Come and do something useful, Stells," says Lucy. We unload the van, lugging big wooden-boxed loudspeakers down a dingy corridor that smells of stale beer and urine. Jeff begins wiring them up onstage. I find myself watching and he starts explaining how they work. 'Pick-ups' on the guitar detect the vibration of the strings, and turn that into an electrical signal, which then goes through foot-operated pedals which enable him to alter it in various ways – he shows me some – then into a 'pre-amplifier', which… It's actually rather interesting, but at that point a bloke with earrings starts bashing a set of drums and drives me away.

38

I stand at the back of the auditorium and watch another guitarist set up. His guitar is hand-painted, has a sticker with *Anarchy* on it, plays the bass notes and is hideously out of tune. Then Lucy struts onto the stage and bellows into a mike.

"One… Two… Is this loud enough? BOLLOCKS!"

There's more noise. The drummer keeps walloping his kit for no apparent reason. Lucy shouts "Arseholes!" down the mike. Jeff tunes the other guitarist's instrument for him (without a tuner; he has perfect pitch). Lucy downs a pint of beer.

"Everyone ready?" Lucy finally calls out. *One Night Flop.* One, two, three, f – !"

"Too fast," Jeff interrupts.

"It's punk!"

"It's still too fast. One. Two. Three. Four."

Oh, lord! Lucy's 'singing'! The sheer racket of the drums. The bass, all over the place. Jeff can actually play, jolly well, it seems to me though I'm no expert on this type of music, but there is a rage in it that I can hardly bear. And the volume!

"How did it sound?" he asks me at the end.

"L – loud."

"Perfect!" says Lucy.

Jeff suggests they practice another number. Lucy tries to put him off – practicing is for hippy musos – but he insists. At the last gig, they totally fucked *Charade Parade.*

The noise really is unsupportable for anyone with sensitive hearing, so I sneak off to the Ladies, where I roll up little balls of loo paper and stick them in my ears. When I reappear, the landlord tells the band to stop as people are coming in. We go to the bar, where the drummer starts talking to me. I can't hear a word he's saying, so have to sneak off to the loo again and take the paper *out* of my ears. Then someone starts playing unpleasant pre-recorded music through the loudspeakers, again at a ridiculous level, so I have to go and get more paper…

"Upset stomach," I explain, blushing.

Once, I said. Never again.

We sit in a tiny makeshift dressing room. Lucy tells me to pop out and see how full the bar is; I do, and report back that there's a big crowd (why was she was so insistent that I come?) but they look rather threatening. "Good," she says.

The landlord comes in and tells us it's time to go on.

"Just a minute," says Lucy. "He needs to tune up," she adds, nodding at Jeff, who grimaces. "Make 'em wait," she adds, once the landlord has gone.

Five minutes later, he is back.

"OK, OK," Lucy says. "Stells, go out front and listen. Tell us if anything is wrong."

I nod and obey. This is her world.

"Come on, boys. Slay 'em," she says as I walk out.

I take my place in the crowd. Most of the audience is male, though there are some females. None dressed like me, of course. There's an atmosphere of… At first I think it is aggression, but then I realize it is excitement. The other day, I went to a performance of the *Requiem* at St Martin in the Fields. Waiting for the music to begin was… well, like this. Minus the beer and the noise.

The boys appear, to some applause and some challenging jeers (but I get that. I wouldn't have leapt up from seat N22 in St Martin and shouted 'Come on, do something amazing for me!' but that's what I felt…) They pick up their instruments. Then Lucy struts out from the wings straight to centre stage, grabs the mike and shouts "'Allo" in a jubilant and totally fake Sarf London voice. Jeff starts tapping his foot and is just about to count the band in, but Lucy beats him to it at about twice the speed.

The trouble is, Lucy is rather good. Dreadful, musically, of course, but she has a kind of presence. I can think of few things I would like to do less than get up in front of a crowd of people and sing (or, in her case, bellow). Lucy struts round the stage, yelling into the microphone, swigging from a pint glass, filling the entire venue with her angst and her rage and her pain and her desire and her sheer bloody alive-ness, and everyone (apart from me) drinks it in.

I'm not secretly envious, honest. But my ears soon start to hurt, so after a few numbers, I retire to the van – Jeff said I should keep the key – and stretch out across the seats. The jangle in my head slowly subsides. Before I know it, it's gone 11.00 and the audience is leaving. I head back in and help the boys dismantle the equipment while Lucy talks to the landlord. They seem to be having some sort of argument about money.

"How did it sound?" Jeff asks me again.

"OK." Then I feel bad about such dishonesty. "It was loud. Especially the singing and the bass."

To me this imbalance had been obvious, but Jeff looks at me with surprise. "I'll get Earl to turn down. Not sure there's a lot I can do about that sister of yours – but it's better to have vocals too loud than too low. We musos hate it, but the punters have come to hear songs, not admire our playing. I'll have a word with whoever is doing the mixing, though. We'll get it better for you next time."

I nod. There won't, of course, be a next time.

Soon we have the van loaded up. Lucy turns to me. "You drive, don't you, Stells?"

"You know I do." (I passed first time.)

"And you've got the key. Come on…"

Jeff nods enthusiastically.

"You were driving earlier…" I tell him.

He grins. "Somebody had to."

*

It turns out that none of them has a valid license. Well, I can't have them getting arrested for driving around illegally, can I?

And, OK, it's nice to have something to belong to. Not exactly 'me', but… well, what does that mean, anyway?

I learn to bring proper ear plugs to gigs, but still often end up sitting in the van reading or listening to music.

On one such occasion, I'm in the van when I notice someone peering in through the passenger-side window. It's Jeff. I switch the music off at once and grin at him nervously.

"Don't stop that, Stella. It's good. Mozart's *Requiem*, isn't it? The Requiem in D minor… Great key." He has his guitar with him, and he carefully places his fingers on the neck then bashes out the chord in a staccato pattern. "Angry and sad."

"You… like Mozart?" I ask.

"Oh, yes. I did unspeakable things to one of the poor man's flute concertos when I was a lad. But it was too hard for me, or I was too lazy, or I fell in love with the blues – I can't remember. I never mastered it, anyway. But I got close enough to realize how beautiful it was."

"Gosh. So how come you play…?" My voice dies.

"Punk? I love it. Aren't I allowed to love more than one kind of music?"

"Well, er, yes. Of course you are. I just… I mean…"

Jeff seems to be enjoying my embarrassment. "You're a strange one, aren't you, Stella? You roll along like a big, deep river."

"Do I?"

He nods. "I wonder what's going on beneath the surface." He starts strumming the guitar again, and I soon recognize the song as *Moon River*. It starts as a kind of send-up, but the longer he plays, the more he gets involved with it.

"That was lovely," I say afterwards.

He looks embarrassed. "Thank you, Stella. It is rather good, isn't it? Henry Mancini. Not cool. But you're right." He strums one of the chords, this time letting it ring. "F sharp minor 7 flat five. That's gorgeous, isn't it? Gorgeous…"

I nod. He puts a finger to his lips. "Don't tell Earl or your sister. They'd have me thrown out for ideological impurity. They'd be totally fucked, of course – oops, pardon my language – but they'd still do it."

I smile.

Silence falls, but it's a friendly, unforced silence. "Cigarette?" he asks.

"No, thanks."

"Didn't think you would."

I don't want him to think I'm completely unadventurous. "I used to. When I was a student."

"*Gauloises*?"

"How did you know?"

"Just guessed."

I feel a bit narked, but don't know what to say. He starts noodling round on his guitar. I don't want the conversation to end. "I… like your guitar. It's smart. Not like Earl's tatty old thing."

His face lights up. "It's a Fender Telecaster. The greatest guitar ever made."

"Why?" I ask. A good Philosopher's question.

"Wilko Johnson plays one."

"Who's he?"

"Who's Wilko Johnson? Stella, we must broaden your musical education!"

I learn all about a band called 'Dr Feelgood', and the 'machine gun' rhythm patterns used by their guitarist, Wilko Johnson, who is Jeff's hero (along with various people, half of whom I've never heard of and, no, he insists, he really means this, Mozart) and is the true father of British punk. The patterns are best done on the Telecaster because of the tightness of the action, which sounds rather rude but is actually about how close the strings are to the neck. "You can put your whole self into it," he says, scrunches up his face and plays one of his furious rhythms. "Everyone goes on about Les Pauls, but… No way."

I grin, though I have no idea what Les Paul has or why people should go on about it.

He grins back. "Here, have a feel."

"You don't mind?"

"I trust you, Stella. You're not the kind of idiot who goes round smashing musical instruments."

He hands me the guitar. I push down on a string and feel a tiny moment of wonder. Could I make music?

Then I hear Lucy. "We're on again, Jeff! Stop trying to get off with my sister."

"*Ein Führerbefehl*," says Jeff. "See you later."

He has a long-standing girl-friend back in Belfast, by the

way.

*

Well, I'm part of the band, now, so I ought to tell you about the rest of us.

1. Lucy (a.k.a. Anne T Social) (vocals) (of a sort, anyway) She's attracted all the attention since she was born, so enough about her.

2. Jeff Spiteful (guitar) That's not his real name, by the way; it's McFadden. But you've met him already. And I'm still a bit annoyed he was such a smart-arse about my *Gauloises*, so enough of him, too.

3. Trucker Tel (drums) Tel is the oldest member of the band. Jeff found him through an ad in Lucy's beloved *New Musical Express*. He can actually drive lorries, but got himself banned a while back – he won't say why. He also finds us most of our work, as he's played all the venues before in groups of various types: trad, pop, psychedelic, rock, funk (see: I'm picking up the terminology). "I'll play anything," he says.

He has a similar attitude to women. If anyone disappears with the hungry-eyed girls who sometimes come backstage after our gigs, it's the Trucker.

"They just like me," he explains one evening. "There's not much competition, either."

"That's a little unfair," I reply.

He shrugs. "Underneath it all, Jeff is a nice Protestant boy who wants True Love and won't settle for anything less. Earl has already found his True Love, himself. You and Luce seem to be straight. So that leaves good old Tel." He chuckles, then adds, "You don't say much about your love life, do you Stella? Is there some bloke lurking in the background? I think you have a long-standing relationship with a professor of Ancient Greek who plays oboe in a classical quintet. Do you write long letters to each other, with fountain pens, on vellum notepaper?"

"I'm between partners," I reply.

4. Earl E Death (bass) Earl is happy to admit he's not very good at playing the bass. "Music isn't about music any longer," he explains. "It's about statement. Image."

Hence, I guess, his uniform of black clothing and dark glasses. He wears the glasses even in the dingiest venues: several times I've seen him trip over pieces of equipment, despite my best attempts to keep the stage tidy. He doesn't eat properly either, with a *penchant* for fast food, which I tell him is not nutritious (he replies that it is contemporary). Hence his sallow look. Or is it more? One day, I voice a suspicion to Lucy, that he might take drugs. She seems to find this incredibly funny.

Earl is impossible to converse with. I'm particularly bad at small talk but he thinks 'serious' conversation is meaningless. "In the modern world, the truly serious person is totally frivolous," he says once.

One evening, however, we're driving back down the M1 from a gig in Stafford. The other three are asleep, Jeff and Tel in the back, Lucy in the front. Earl sits between the Tranter sisters, nodding his head to some inner beat. We pass an accident on the opposite carriageway.

"Those poor people," I say – to myself really, but Earl

picks up on the comment.

"They might have wanted it," he replies. "*Thanatos*. The inner human impulse to self-destruction."

"Freudian theory is self-referential," I riposte. "If you try and criticize it, you are accused of having a hidden psychological agenda."

"Doesn't mean to say it's not right," Earl replies. "You're quite clever, aren't you?"

I'm not having this, even if his point about Freud was rather a good one. "I'm very clever," I reply. "I studied Philosophy. It's the most interesting thing I've ever done."

"Philosophy doesn't get you anywhere, though, does it?"

"I believe it does."

"Oh, you're letting yourself down there, Stella. 'Believe' is a good word for Joe Average, but not for a philosopher. Philosophers need more than belief. They need certainty, don't they? And of course they can't have it. That's what drives them all crazy. They know they can't prove anything. All their clever arguments collapse if you push hard enough."

"That's nihilism."

"Exactly!"

"Doesn't that scare you?"

"It did for a few minutes when I first worked it out. Then I got used to it. Now I embrace it. It's how the world is. All fucked up and nowhere to go."

I pull out to overtake a lorry, pondering as I do so that my skill behind the wheel is not some arbitrary fact in a pointless universe but something which I have taken effort to learn and which is now proving useful to myself and to four other people too. "You really think that?"

"Of course, I do. Don't you?"

"No. I believe one can find a solid point of certainty on which to build a constructive and meaningful life." I begin a potted version of what we learned at The Enlightenment Club.

"Great Art?" Earl cuts in half way through. "What the fuck's that? A load of old stuff touted around by middle-aged middle-class academic types. Is that at the heart of your life, Stella? Really? Honestly?"

"Yes," I say. There is, perhaps, a hint of hesitancy in my voice: with my new role, I have much less time for concerts or serious reading.

Earl shakes his head. "You're fooling yourself, Stella. That stuff is dead – as is all the talk about 'certainty' or 'meaning'. Those are just words that scared, mediocre people make up to make themselves feel better. Whistling in the dark – and a crap tune, too."

"I don't think I could live if I really thought that."

He pauses. "No, you probably couldn't."

Then, as suddenly as he entered the conversation, he disengages. By the next junction (number 12, the A5120, which means there are 36 miles to go), he is asleep.

Philosophy, Great Art and the City: Love

I meant what I said about not having time for serious art. But one day at work Caitlin, one of the solicitors – the brightest, people say – mentions that she rehearses with a choir. Guess what piece they are working on at the moment!

"Could I come and listen?" I ask eagerly.

"You can come and sing if you want."

"Oh, no, I don't think I could do that. I can't read music."

She shrugs. "You'll pick it up. Just open and close your mouth to start with; soon you'll be singing along with the rest of us."

"I'd be… embarrassed," I add.

She gives me a sceptical look.

She's right, of course. I buy a score, a book on how to read music and a Stylophone, a toy keyboard with a picture of Rolf Harris on the packaging. Every evening I work through a section of the score, grab a meal, do another section… Twelve pages a week, I need to master.

I'm a jellyfish before my first rehearsal, but the moment the music begins I'm strong again. All that work has paid off: the woman next to me is even impressed by my singing. This is *my* music. My Mohican, my nose-stud, my Fender Telecaster.

I meet Malcolm at the second rehearsal.

It's a muggy evening. We do the *Dies Irae;* near the end, there's a judgement-day clap of thunder and when we leave it's coming down in buckets. An old man offers me a lift to the tube. I accept. We get into one of those cars with wood panelling on the outside, and talk about the piece as we inch along the road, which has become flooded. Wolfgang Amadeus jumps up and down in my head like the rain that is bouncing off the car's bonnet and hammering down on its echoing metal roof.

Di-es ir-ae, di-es il-la.

Above the racket, my companion starts telling me that bits were written by a pupil of Mozart's called Francis Xavier Sussmayr, or at least finished by Sussmayr from notes Mozart left. He often tries to work out which bits are which – the *Sanctus* drags a bit so is probably not the maestro's. Of course, there is a letter dated the eighth of February 1800 in which Sussmayr claims to have written certain sections, but this has to be taken with a pinch of salt as he was short of money and trying to claim royalty payments on the piece, so…

We're at the tube station. He indicates to pull in and a flipper pops out of the side of the car.

"I'm Malcolm Stringer, by the way."

I fiddle in my bag and eventually find one of my

Stella Tranter

Flat 6

32 Eaglescliffe Road

LONDON W12

cards with the book and the treble clef on.

"Nice card. And nice to meet you, Stella," he continues, giving my hand a perfect shake: firm but not crushing; long enough to be sincere but not too long as to be clingy or lecherous. Then I dash out into the rain. I'm soaked in the twenty or so feet between the car and the tube entrance, but feel warm and cheerful inside.

At the next rehearsal, we find ourselves in the coffee queue together. Malcolm says that since our conversation he's done more research on Mozart and Francis Xavier Sussmayr, and that the experts now reckon Mozart wrote all the tunes but Sussmayr did some of the orchestration. If I listen to the *Communio* I'll find…

I suddenly feel a yawn coming on, and force my face into a series of increasingly weird expressions to prevent it, until I'm faced with a simple choice: give in or dislocate my jaw.

"You're not really interested, are you?" says Malcolm.

"No, it's just… I was up rather late last night. Working on the score," I add, in case he thinks I lead a life of unremitting hedonism.

He nods, unconvinced, and I grin back helplessly. End of friendship, I guess. Shame…

"Would you care to have dinner with me one evening next week?" he asks.

*

"So, how was your big date?"

Well, I had to tell Lucy. It's the day after the dinner, and she is debriefing me.

"Nice."

She grimaces. "I hate that word."

"OK. It was wonderful. It was a lovely restaurant. Very unassuming on the outside. Inside – class. They really cared about the food. The waiter went on about the regions of France each dish came from. The wines – "

"So it was expensive, then?"

"I guess it was."

"And what was grandpa like?"

"Don't call him that. He was very interesting. He's been

51

to all sorts of unusual places. He's an engineer. Worked in Panama, Thailand, Arabia, Egypt – "

"Helped build the pyramids, did he?"

"Lucy, he's sixty-two. That's the prime of life for some people."

She grimaces again.

"Anyway, older men are more interesting," I continue. "Maybe your musician friends are more fun – Jeff's rather a sweetie underneath it all – but most of the young ones I meet…" I grimace. "They are rather dull. Callow."

"You choose them, Stells. 'Someone with real prospects', you say, then you come back complaining they just talked about lawsuits or share prices. But we're getting off the point. Tell me more about Bus Pass Boy."

"Not if you take the mickey out of him."

"Nobody says 'taking the mickey' any longer, Stells."

"I do."

She grins. "So you had this slap-up meal…"

"We enjoyed French provincial cuisine. And the conversation with it was… grown up. We talked about ourselves a bit – he actually listened to what I had to say; how's that for a man? We talked about art. Music – classical music of course. Philosophy."

Lucy grins. "Stells, he's perfect for you."

"Not really. He's married."

*

But we do keep on seeing each other. It just feels so pleasant. I tell myself we're just friends, so what's the problem? He gets precious little friendship from his wife, who doesn't share his interest in Great Art or Philosophy. They lead very different lives: she spends all her time in a 'place'

52

they have in Hampshire, where she gardens and plays bridge with other middle-aged ladies.

Then one evening he invites me round to dinner. He has a flat in a nice street in Bayswater, full of genuine oil-paintings and antique furniture. We sit in lush armchairs and talk over a glass of sherry. He makes a casserole with a delicious rich gravy and we talk over that. We talk over the summer pudding and over the Quinta da Foz and Stilton. Then our eyes meet…

"Stella, dear, an old man like me has no right to ask anything of a vibrant young lady like you," he says. "But I am completely enchanted by you. I ask you for the chance for us to be more than friends."

I burble some sort of reply.

He grasps my hand and puts it to his lips. "I would like the honour of being your lover," he goes on. "I will totally understand if you say that is not your wish, and shall not mention the subject again."

"It… is my wish," I manage, realizing as I say so quite how much I mean this. "V – very much. But… I'm a little nervous."

"We can take as long as you need," he says, with a broad grin. "Time is our servant, not our master."

"No. Let's… get on with it!" I blurt out. A chorus of critical voices spring up in my head. Hussy! Adulterer! I shove them all to one side, and squeeze his hand.

"We shall be beautiful and glorious," he says. "Like the music we both love. Well, you will be beautiful, anyway, Stella. I shall just be blissfully happy."

I try and bat the compliment away, then stop myself. He reaches out and strokes my hair (my hopeless, uncontrollable hair…)

*

"Can he get it up?" asks Lucy when she forces the truth out of me (she says she 'can tell').

"None of your business. But, yes. Several times, actually."

"Oh. Good for him. Do you love him? Does your life divide into two parts? Part one is before you met, a rehearsal in someone's garage. Part two, after, is the live gig. Full house, crazy fucking audience, adrenalin pumping so hard you wish you could fly…"

"I'm not sure I'd put it like that. But, yes, I suppose I do."

*

Christmas is painful. No Malcolm, just family and Lucy's latest boyfriend – I can't even remember his name, but he's a music journalist of some kind – and comments from Mother about how nice he is and isn't it about time… I even have to unwrap Malcolm's present upstairs, to keep it a secret. Lucy, of course, finds out anyway and gets a fit of the giggles.

"It's a bit of old pottery!"

"It's Egyptian. From the reign of Queen Tawosaret, around 1185 BC. Malcolm found it in the desert."

"That's cultural theft!"

"Well, maybe. But nobody else cared for it, and it was special to him. And now he's given it to me. Here, touch it. Isn't it wonderful? It makes me think of giant temples, sacred cats on cushions embroidered with spun gold, women with snakey eyes, the sound of huge trumpets made from the horns of now-extinct beasts. Wooo-oo-oo…"

She runs purple-nailed fingers over it. "It makes me think of the council rubbish tip," she says.

54

*

I usually wait for Malcolm to contact me between what he calls our 'assignations'. He does so, most days. We chat about art, music and philosophy but also about little things we've seen, done or felt. It feels so natural, so right, so clear.

One week the phone doesn't ring. I tell myself there must be a good reason. We've an assignation for Saturday, anyway. He'll cook lunch, then we'll have coffee and brandy, and then off to his bedroom, where I am now perfectly happy to 'disrobe' in front of him. Hell, no, I enjoy it.

On Friday evening, I'm pottering around the flat, listening to Beethoven's violin concerto. The phone rings. It'll be him!

"Er, Hello, is that Stella Tranter?"

"Yes."

"Er, I'm a friend of Malcolm Stringer's. Roy Gault."

"Oh, yes. He's spoken about you." I don't get to meet Malcolm's friends, as they all know Leticia too.

"He asked me to tell you that he's had a problem and can't make your…. appointment on Saturday. A family thing – he'd have contacted you himself, but he's a bit, well, busy."

"Busy?"

"His son's been in a road accident."

He doesn't really get on with his son, Colin, who's a rather wild character. "Oh," I say.

"It's nasty. Malcolm needs to spend some time with him and Leticia. He said you'd understand."

"Yes, of course," I say breezily. "Er, did he say when he'd be able to contact me?"

"He said he'd be in touch when he could. It wasn't anything important, was it?"

None of your business. "Naaah," I think I say, off-handed, casual. (The reality is probably a rather panicked 'No!')

*

The letter arrives a few days later.

…Suddenly realized the importance of family after all… Will always treasure the memories of our time together… Feel sure you will take this in a philosophical spirit…

"No!" This one is a scream.

I rip it to shreds, try and stick the shreds together again, get Sellotape stuck to my fingers, sit in the middle of my room weeping, grab a coat, run down the stairs, pound furiously round the streets of London W12 then realize I'm lost. Luckily, a cab appears and I flag it down.

"Actually, you can stop here," I tell the driver when we get to the off-licence at the foot of Eaglescliffe Road.

Next day, I'm late for work. Mr Prendergast snaps at me and I snap back. Caitlin hears this, and comes to have a chat with me. I tell her what's happened, and she starts going on about being positive and looking for silver linings. She then 'puts a word in for me' (a week or so later, I get a 'warning', but nothing further is said).

I call Lucy that evening, and she comes over and insists on taking me out. I suddenly want to go dancing: I don't know why, as I don't really like disco music, but I want to lose myself in something. I do, and some of the pain disappears.

Lucy isn't a great disco fan, either, though she grudgingly admits it's popular with Black and gay people so must have something to it. It's sweet of her to play along. We end up back at the flat, with more – and better quality – wine, and she lets me drone on about Malcolm.

"He's only a bloke, Stells," she breaks in finally.

"He respected me!" I cry.

"Till he dumped you, yes."

"No. He had no choice. There are rules, Lucy."

"For some people…"

I sigh. "He understood me!"

"Well, find someone else who understands you."

"There seem to be so few people who do."

Lucy nods. "Well, you are a bit odd." As she says this, a chain between her nose stud and the safety-pin in her left ear rattles. "Go and get laid, anyway. It's what I always do. Get back on your horse."

"I don't have a horse to get back on to."

Lucy reaches over and gives me a big hug. "You need to toughen up, Stells. Shall I pop out and get another bottle?"

*

I go to a recital by an up-and-coming young flautist at the Wigmore Hall: after the first piece I turn to the complete stranger next to me and say, "That was so elegant, wasn't it, darling?"

Well, it's what I've got used to. I disappear at the interval, and can't face concerts after that.

Philosophy? I can't summon up the concentration. The books sit around with the markers in the same places they were a week ago, a month ago.

I have Wolfgang Amadeus, Élisabeth-Louise and the Countess, of course, but they have started staring at me and asking difficult questions. 'We are who we are,' they say. 'Who are you?'

There's still the band, too – but they seem to be doing fewer gigs. One Saturday, they have one at the Hope and

Anchor in Islington. Jeff insists everyone rehearse for it. "We've been getting sloppy," he says. Grudgingly, the rest agree, and we convene at midday.

"I've got a new song," says Jeff. He sits down, begins strumming and sings. It's rather lovely, a ballady sort of thing. Is that an F sharp minor 7 flat 5 in there? It's for Annie back in Belfast, of course.

"Cool singing," says Lucy. "But does it fits our – "

"It's shite," Earl cuts in.

Jeff turns and glares at him.

"Radio Two shite," Earl goes on.

"Oh, yeah. You know so much about music!"

Earl just sneers. "Middle class shite," he adds.

"Well, Earl, you certainly know all about being middle class, don't you?" Jeff fires back. "Remind me; which minor public school did you attend? Mummy and daddy were so keen for little Edward to get on in the world, weren't they? I bet they were the talk of the Conservative Club for weeks when you got into Buggerhurst or whatever it was called. Did they make you Head Boy there?"

Earl pauses for a moment, then advances towards him, fists clenched. He's wearing his shades, so he trips over a lead and tumbles forward. Jeff laughs and holds out a hand to help him, but Earl appears to misinterpret this, as he grabs hold of Jeff's legs and makes him lose his balance.

Jeff topples into his speaker stack. "My guitar!" he calls out.

The Telecaster looks OK to me, but Jeff turns ice cold. He stands up, very slowly. He hands the guitar to Lucy, who's watching the proceedings with mounting interest. He rolls up his sleeves.

"You… could… have… damaged… my… guitar," he says.

"It looks OK…" Earl replies, getting to his feet and starting to retreat. This time he treads on one of Jeff's foot-pedals and tumbles into the drum kit, which dissolves with a cacophony of crashing cymbals, sticks tumbling out of a holder and the floor tom-tom falling over. He grabs a now empty cymbal stand and tries to defend himself with it.

"Chaps, stop!" I say. "This isn't very nice! I think you really ought to be a bit more sensible and – "

Jeff yanks the stand out of Earl's hands. "If anything's happened to my guitar, I'm going to redecorate your poncy, pretentious little face in a way that will never recover."

He jabs Earl with one end of the stand; at this point, Tel gets off his drum stool, steps across his fallen hi-hat and places himself between the combatants.

"Lads…" he says.

Just that. *Lads…*

Both look at him, then at the ground. Earl heads off to the toilet; Jeff shakes himself down and walks across to Lucy to collect the Telecaster and double-check it for damage.

The gig that evening is rather good, actually, but it's the last one that we do.

*

Lucy soon finds a new musical direction.

"I'm a New Romantic," she tells me.

"I'm an Old Romantic," I reply, remembering when Malcolm and I went to Frinton-on-Sea for a weekend.

"You must come to the Blitz Club. It's cool."

We go.

"Perhaps I was a punk after all," I say to myself as I sip

an absurdly expensive cocktail. Lucy soon hooks up with a young man who looks like he's on his way to a fancy dress party dressed as a pirate. I get a cab home.

I'm late again next morning. Mr Prendergast calls me in and tells me I'm fired. I want to reply that I didn't want to work in his stupid little firm anyway. Now belatedly aware of my true punk identity, I want to tell him that the law is a middle-class plot against truth, authenticity, honesty and beauty, and, quite frankly, he can shove it up his bloody arse.

"I'm sorry things didn't work out," I say.

*

"I'm giving notice to quit."

"That's a shame, Miss Tranter. You've been a model tenant. Is there anything we've done wrong?"

"No. I just don't want to live in Central London any longer."

"Oh dear. Last time we spoke you said how wonderful it was. All that culture."

"I'm fed up with culture. It hasn't helped me with my life at all."

"It's never done a lot for me. Unless you include country and western music, which I don't think you do, do you?"

"Not really."

"Going anywhere exciting?"

"Just back home."

Sydenham or Penge East?

I'll decide when I get there.

*

Lucy helps me move. The pirate is too busy to join us, or maybe he has a wooden leg and would have problems with the stairs. She hires a van with a driver, a wiry, studious-looking young man who tells me proudly as he lugs another box of books into the van that he is a novelist.

"Wow," I reply. "What have you written?"

"Nothing."

Lucy has a kind of snigger she does when people say something really stupid.

"Yet," he adds quickly.

When the van is loaded, I pop back upstairs, officially to check if we've left anything behind, but actually to sit on the floor, gaze round at the empty shelves and the black rectangles where Wolfgang Amadeus, Élizabeth-Louise and the Countess were, and remember what it felt like to dream of finding love as a Philosopher and Lover of Great Art in the Big City.

At the end of Möricke's novella, Eugenie, one of the young women in the family that the Mozarts descended on was left in an empty room, too. The genius had moved on and would never return. The last line: 'the bitter tears began to fall'.

Mine do, too.

Reverend, Discreet, Advised and Sober

I'm happy.

No, really, I am. I have a lovely little one-bedroom flat, near Penge East station, and a job in Ladywell. Well, Lewisham, actually, but Ladywell sounds so much nicer. The Big City is a strange dream I had a long time ago.

I keep the décor bright. Simple, rather stylized pictures of landscapes (I think they're of Italy, but I'm not sure). The old ones felt pretentious somehow, and I got rid of them (even Élisabeth-Louise and her hat, whom I still miss a little). And today I'm finally having a clear-out of the cardboard boxes that have been sitting in a corner since I moved in. There's a charity shop round the corner.

On the way there, I trip over an uneven paving stone and suddenly I'm sprawled on the pavement with a load of books spewed out in front of me.

"Are you OK?"

I look up to see a stocky, youngish man in a pair of cords and a lumberjack shirt. He holds out a hand, which I take to get myself up to my feet.

"Can I help?"

"That's most kind."

We begin picking up the books. *Discourse on Method. Principia Ethica. The Birth of Tragedy from the Spirit of Music.*

"Weren't you at Sydenham School?" he asks.

"Yes," I reply hesitantly.

"I was at the College. We did some art thing with you once." He stares up at the sky and starts flicking his finger. "Lucy. That's it. Lucy… Gotta help me out here."

"Tranter. You're mistaking me for my sister."

"Oh, right. I'm sorry. You do look alike, though."

"I'm fatter and my hair is incapable of keeping any shape. Though it is its natural colour: hers was probably bright green or something at the time."

"Probably. That art thing was a bit… different." He puts *A Student's Guide to Sartre* into the box. "Let me carry this… So, you still live round here?" he adds, as we approach the shop.

"Yes."

"Me too. Anything else to carry?" he adds as we walk out again.

"There's a couple of boxes of records."

"You must let me. I'm Bobby, by the way. Bobby Mowatt."

"Oh, I'm Stella. Stella Tranter, obviously. Well, no, not obviously, is it? I could have married. But I've never really… I'm not very…"

We head back to my flat, and he waits politely outside while I fetch the biggest box, which he then takes.

"Oof – that's heavy. Replacing them all with these new CD thingies?"

"Not really. I just – I don't know – went off music."

He nods thoughtfully. "Never really been my cup of tea, the classical stuff, anyway."

We make the journey to the shop without incident, then hover while the assistant flicks through the items.

"Philosophy books and classical music on vinyl don't fetch much," she says, and offers me £5 for the lot. It doesn't seem nearly enough, but I'm not carrying it back to the flat.

"Worth a tenner, surely?" Bobby puts in.

"Seven pounds fifty…"

"It was very nice of you to help," I tell Bobby when we're back out in the street.

"No problem." He looks at me with a new intensity. "You don't fancy, er, meeting up for dinner sometime, do you? On me, of course."

"Not really."

He looks hurt.

"Sorry. That sounds horrible. I don't really go out. It never seems to work and – I'm really rather happy on my own."

"Oh. Shame. Well, if you change your mind… Here's my card."

*

A few days later, I'm in the flat ironing, and suddenly think this refusing to go out is ridiculous. I rush over to my handbag and dig out the card.

Robert Mowatt
Assistant Director
Mowatt Plastics
Unit 5B
Minerva Industrial Estate
Croydon

There's a number, too.

I cross to the phone, dial most of the number, wonder what the smell is, rush across to the ironing board, shrug – they weren't very nice jeans, anyway – go back to the phone…

*

When Bobby and I meet, I make a little speech about not being much cop at 'dating' and really only looking for friendship, is that OK? He says that's fine; friendship is good.

We start going to the cinema, alternating between action movies and more romantic ones.

At Christmas, Bobby asks me to the Rotary Club annual dinner/dance. I want to look good for this, and spend a fortune on an outfit. When I get it home, I try it on again and it suddenly looks grotesque. I contemplate returning it, but can't find the receipt, unlike a hoard of other receipts that I immediately find: for a coffee and Danish at Sam's Breakfast Bar, for a book called *Get over your Past and Live a Bright New Future*, for another coffee and Danish at Sam's, for a chocolate and cream special – oh, bugger the receipts.

The day before, I spend another fortune on getting my hair done. And then it's the evening itself! I put the outfit on and stare at myself in the mirror. It looks OK. So does my hair: maybe the problem is that I never spend enough money on it usually. With some nice earrings and a few touches of make-up – hell, I'm going to enjoy myself!

I take a taxi – another extravagance. The venue is one of these outer London hotels which was a Victorian country house till suburbia flooded past it. But it can still put on a show. There are torches lining the stairs to the lobby, where I find Bobby waiting, looking terribly dapper in his black tie, DJ and cummerbund. He tells me I look 'marvellous' and leads me through to a dome-ceilinged dining room which is already buzzing with conversation.

We are on a table with eight other people, including someone called Bill Carr, who's some big cheese in Rotary and a few years older than Bobby, and his wife Matilda, whom I seem to recognize.

"Yes!" she says when I ask her if she was at Sydenham School. "I remember you, too. You were a bit of a rebel, weren't you? Did lots of art. Didn't you dye your hair blue once?"

I smile. "We all have our little moments of rebellion." Well, why not?

After a three-course dinner, a jazz band comes on. They are awful. The bassist keeps losing the time, the trumpeter splits loads of notes, the drums are too loud, and the singer is probably the second worst vocalist I've ever heard.

Never mind: Bobby orders another bottle of red (it's not great, but stuff at hotels rarely is, is it?). And then, joy of joys, the band finally finishes.

"Round of applause for the Sydenham Stompers. Weren't they great?"

Everyone else claps enthusiastically. I join in a bit, as I don't want to stand out.

"More!" people begin to shout. I suddenly take an interest in wine, as I'm not going along with that.

"We've got a tight schedule, I'm afraid," the master of ceremonies carries on. Thank God, I think. "I'm Vince Bland and I'm here to take you through to midnight with the latest hits and some golden oldies. Any requests?"

Packing all that noisy stuff away and letting human beings converse rather than being deafened?

Oh, don't be such a frump, Stella. It's nice to be here. To belong, for a few hours anyway…

The music begins and I find myself tapping my foot along to it. (Why not? It's in time. It's properly balanced. The vocalists can actually sing…)

"Aaaah!" That *Le Freak* thing comes on. I glance at Bobby, who is deep in conversation with Bill about the new Labour leader, Neil Kinnock, and whether he would be any less dangerous than his predecessor.

"Do you want to dance?" I ask him.

He looks paralyzed with indecision.

"Go on, Bobby," says Bill. "We're here to enjoy ourselves!"

I take Bobby's hand and lead him out onto floor. I begin to move to the music – he does too, a bit. Then suddenly it takes possession of me, just like it did that evening after Malcom and I split up. I welcome it. Totally. Why not? I leap up and down. I shake my hips. Yes!!! I wave my hair around, undoing all that money spent on it – but it feels good. What's money, compared to this? Bobby stops jiggling about and seems to catch some of my energy. In the middle bit where the strings keep going up and up, he starts jerking his knees from side to side and flapping his arms in the air. It's like a duck trying to climb a ladder. But it's a cute duck, an underneath-its-formal-plumage-rather-vulnerable duck.

More up-tempo numbers follow – I want to dance to them all! – then the lights go down and the songs get slow. I want Bobby to hold me close, and he does. I want him to kiss me. With a little encouragement, he does. I want…

We go back to his afterwards for a coffee (even though we've had it poured down our throats all evening, the weapons-grade stuff that even posh venues seem to specialize in). As he disappears into his kitchen, I think for a moment of Malcolm, then give a shrug.

Bobby returns, and heads towards an empty chair (I am on the sofa). I pat the space beside me.

*

There are fewer people on my side of the aisle than Bobby's – Mother says that shows what a catch Bobby is. On

67

my team, there's Mother, Mr Brown (Jacqui and her husband Paul, who is 'something in sales', are away on holiday, fortunately), Aunt Alice and her carer Grace, a girl called Vee who I was at Upper Norwood with, a work colleague called Tracey (I'm accountant /office manager in Happy Daze, the travel agency in the High Street) and of course Lucy, with the aspiring novelist, whom she's now sort-of dating (they have an 'open relationship'). She says marriage is 'bourgeois', but has actually been a brick, organizing all sorts of things and taking me out to get drunk one evening to celebrate 'the end of my freedom'. Father is not here: mother insisted it was impossible to contact him, and I gave in. Maybe it was even true.

"Holy matrimony is an honourable estate, instituted of God in the time of man's innocence, which is commended of Saint Paul to be honourable among all men, and therefore is not by any to be enterprised nor taken in hand unadvisedly, lightly or wantonly, but reverently, discreetly, advisedly, soberly…"

As the vicar intones those words, I know this is not the end of my freedom but its beginning. A weight is slipping from around my shoulders, like an albatross in a poem I once read. I was lousy at being a teenager and a 'young adult' (which I now realize means 'overgrown teenager'). Now I'm moving to the stage that truly matters, proper adulthood. All that other stumbling, solitary stuff was just a preparation for this: real life.

"…and in the fear of God, into which holy estate these two persons present now come to be joined. Therefore if any man can show any just cause, why they may not lawfully be joined together, let him now speak, or forever hold his peace."

Nobody will speak, of course, but we still both glance round at the congregation. I suddenly notice two men have slipped into an empty pew at the back. One is wearing a huge white collar and has long, curly hair; the other is rather Germanic-looking and has a walrus moustache. Are they about to object?

Silly question; it's just a trick of the light – the bright, fresh light that's shining in through the nave windows onto two future lives that have begun here today.

Interlude 2

I've been married six years and three months. We have no children: I'm not sure why. Maybe neither of us wanted them enough. Our social life is quiet, too. I'd rather hoped it would take off, with a circle of interesting friends, but, well, it just hasn't. That's fine, really. I'm not the madly social type. I take a quiet interest in the business, though manufacturing is not my skillset. Bobby's brother runs it with him, and he made it very clear from early on that he didn't want me getting involved at any serious level. It would 'upset the balance of things'. Bobby, bless him, tried to fight my corner, but George was adamant. I was annoyed at the time, but things move on. I still think they take on too much debt, but, as I say, that's not my area of expertise.

It's my 35th birthday in just over a week. We have a little advance celebration, as Bobby has to be at Plastex '90 in Pittsburgh on the actual day. I went with him to the first of these conventions, but didn't really fit in… His mum and dad bring a bottle of Champagne. We all sit in the garden, which is looking lovely, and drink it. Old Mr Mowatt says: "Big milestone, 35. Back in the old days, that was the half-way point."

"Half way point of what?" I say, rather more snappily than I'd like. Reg irritates me, though I don't know why (which makes me feel bad about being irritated, which in turn makes me feel even worse.)

"Life."

I rein in a comment about not planning to die aged 70

and say, "Gosh. I hadn't thought of that."

*

The Big Day itself dawns early with a call at 4.30 in the morning. "It's what? Oh, I'm sorry – I thought it would be much later. I never get this dashed international clock stuff right… Anyway, happy birthday, darling."

I go back to sleep and get up late – I've taken the day off. I treat myself to a bottle of Waitrose freshly-squeezed orange with my breakfast. Then I go for a long walk round the old Crystal Palace. At first, I feel the simple exhilaration of being out in the fresh air, but soon this isn't enough. Half-way point or not, I want this day to be significant. I want something amazing to happen.

I get to the point where you can see the roofs of the Poly (or the University of Catford as it is now). I find myself remembering that study group – what was it called again? I see the old tape-recorder, the eager faces of the students. I can even smell the books. Whatever happened to Anna? A strain of music comes back to me. Mozart's *Requiem*, wasn't it?

I'm right at the top of the hill now, and pause to gaze down at the sports pitches, the traffic doing battle with the South Circular Road, a train pulling out of Sydenham Hill station. Rows of houses stretch away towards the North Downs. Nice, sensible properties: ours went up by £15,000 last year (though much of that has disappeared into a new mortgage).

Suddenly their sameness is horrifying. What do they do to the individual human beings who get squeezed into them? *In their heart, everyone knows they are a unique being, only once on this earth…*

Ah, yes, that quote. Nietzsche, wasn't it? An intense,

71

hyper-critical bookworm who knew nothing of real life. He never married. He may never even have had sex (not that I do that much now, but you don't after a few years, do you?) I seem to remember he had a kind of girlfriend / Muse called Lou Andreas-Salomé, but she wouldn't sleep with him. Not surprising, with that ridiculous moustache of his.

I find myself laughing, not just at Nietzsche's moustache and how poor old Lou must have dreaded kissing him, but at myself and my ridiculous youthful enthusiasms. Didn't I even go round in some absurd beret?

Ouch!

Time to head home and get on with the rest of my real life.

Eternal

"Alto… Some experience…." says Gloria.

"It was a while ago that I sang it," I reply. "But know the piece pretty well."

I saw the ad in the local post office, not long after my birthday.

The Sydenham Songbirds
need singers, all voices, for a performance of
The *Requiem* by Wolfgang Amadeus Mozart
Ring Gloria on 081…

Was that some kind of spooky message up there on the common? No, I don't believe in that sort of thing. But the moment I saw the ad, something inside began nagging me.

"…And it's *Mrs* Stella Mowatt?"

"That's right."

For a while, I ignored the nagging, but it just grew more intense. 'Why not give it a try?' became 'You really ought to give it a try' and then 'So, what are you afraid of, then?'

Gloria has a cheerful voice. "It's nice to have some other married ladies on board, Stella. We get an awful lot of unmarrieds looking for husbands and very few eligible men. You can't imagine the problems that can cause!" She laughs. "First rehearsal was last week, but if you know the piece, that shouldn't matter."

"It won't," I say.

*

"I haven't sung this for ages," I tell the women on either

side of me before we start.

"I'd never sung it at all before last week," says the one to my left, who turns out to be a perfect sight-reader. The older one, to my right, is, like me, largely singing from memory. But her memory is much better than mine. I get lost several times: the sight-reader kindly points out where we are, though I sense a rising exasperation in her.

Half way through *Rex Tremendae*, I know. I'll not come back. Last time I sang this, I was single and had time to burn, which I spent wearing flat an old vinyl disk, poring over a score and working out every note. Now I've got a husband, a home, a life.

But I'm glad I accepted the challenge. It's as important to know where you don't fit as to know where you do. We get as far as the end of the *Domine Jesu*, then it's time to snap our folders shut, put them back in the correct pile and go home.

"See you next week, Stella!" chirrups Gloria as we leave.

I grin. I'll give her a call during the week and let her know.

Wolfgang Amadeus has other ideas. He inserts tunes into my brain at every possible moment: at work, in the garden, lying in bed waiting for Bobby to finish the Times crossword. Even shopping…

"Next, please."

Quam olim Abrahae, tiddle pom...

"Next!"

"Oh, sorry."

Promisisti…

Beep

Quam olim Abrahae, tiddle pom…

Beep

Promisisti…

The check-out lady is looking at me very strangely.

"Do you know Mozart's *Requiem*?" I ask her.

"No. What is it?"

"A piece of music."

"Who by?"

"Well, him. Mozart."

Beep.

She shakes her head. "Not heard of them. There's a special offer on these. 2 for 1. Do you want to go and get an extra box?"

"Not to worry. It's really wonderful, you know."

"We like to keep customers happy."

"No. Mozart's *Requiem*. You should give it a try."

Beep.

I'm lucky, to know and love this piece. So make the bloody effort to sing it!

*

The spotlights glint off the instruments in front of us: gold off the brass, mellow off the dark wooden soundboxes of the strings, a flash of silver from the rims of the tympani. Applause breaks out as Joanna, the orchestra leader, takes her seat and builds as Laurence, our conductor, mounts the podium. He gives a flourishing bow, turns, taps his baton twice on his music stand and raises it. The music begins. Slow and stealthy. Then it's two bars till our entry. Then one…

Panic! I'll come in a beat early, and with a hideous noise like something out of The Omen (which Lucy insisted I see back in 1976, and which I still have nightmares about occasionally). Everyone will turn and stare in horror at the monstrosity that has planted itself among their decent human selves.

We all come in together, right time, right note, as sweet as can be. Our voices, united, build slowly up through the *Introit* into the *Kyrie Eleison*. The music grows with us, expanding, like one of those speeded-up films of flowers opening leaf after leaf, welcoming life. Then the *Dies Irae*, and a new metaphor comes unbidden to me. I'm with a mysterious man in a strange place. He walks up to me and kisses me fully on the lips. We begin ripping the clothes off each other, and –

Stella! We're in a church! This is Mozart!

Luckily, the next section begins with just a trombone and a soloist, and my imagination is reined back. As the other soloists enter and begin to trade exquisite melodies, I'm not reminded of anything erotic or even floral. It's rather a relief.

The music flows on: the anguish of *Lacrimosa*; the sudden restless energy of *Domine Jesu*; the gentle *Benedictus*; the triumphal final ascent to *Lux Aeterna,* where Wolfgang Amadeus takes us each individually by the hand and leads us up a golden, angel-lined staircase with huge rococo doors at the top. These fly open, at his command, on the final D chord, and blinding light floods in. Laurence holds and holds the D till our lungs are fit to burst with joy.

Applause is echoing round the building. I want to hug and kiss the singers all around me. We are ordinary people, but together, tonight we have created something truly transcendent.

*

"You looked like you were enjoying yourself," says Bobby as we drive home.

"Oh, yes! It was like… Well, it's hard to say what it was like. How about you?"

76

"Yeah. You know it's not really my cup of tea, classical music, but I didn't get bored. Well, not much."

"Not much?"

"The solo sections were a bit long. But when you lot were letting rip – it sounded good." We join a queue of cars. "These wretched lights! They only let about five cars through at a time. We're on the South Circular, for heaven's sake, not some B-road. Europe's other capital cities have proper traffic management systems!"

We don't really talk about the concert after that.

*

There's an excellent write-up in the Gazette. I buy a scrapbook and glue the review in next to a flier and Bobby's programme and ticket, which I rescued from the waste paper bin. I ponder what transcendent music will fill the rest of the pages.

A few weeks later, a letter comes: we've been asked to repeat the performance at St Jude's church, Ingelow, as part of a music festival. There's no money. Ingelow is up on the East Coast somewhere, so it will be quite a journey there and back. The orchestra is made up of local amateurs, and may not be much good. Would I be interested?

Of course!

I suggest to Bobby we make a weekend of it.

"You go and have a sing," he says. "I'll stay here and get some serious golf in."

I nod. Couldn't he have taken up a more interesting sport? I rather like cricket: it's elegant and slow-paced. Or something we could do together. Badminton? Oh, well…

*

"As far as we know, St Jude's was commenced in 1317.

You can still see traces of Early English in the north aisle."

I'm trapped.

"The transept windows take the simpler lancet form, which soon evolved into the more sophisticated arches of the Decorated period."

Helplessly trapped.

"Then along came the Black Death, which put a stop to church building for a long time. A blessing in disguise, of course, as church architecture had evolved considerably by the time building was recommenced."

I nod. A disease so horrific that it killed half the population but it got this old bore's church looking nicer, so that was OK. I wonder if I could get a tiny bacillus and drop it in his wine.

You're a guest, Stella. Be nice.

We came up on the coach today and have already had a sing-through in St Jude's, the church where we'll be performing tomorrow. It sounded a bit rough, but we have the day to sort things out. We're now at a reception in someone's house.

"Of course the actual glass is undistinguished," my captor drones on. "Cromwell destroyed the original with his usual thoroughness, and the Victorian replacements lack originality. The apse is of similar mediocrity. The rood-screen has – "

"Hello, George." A new person joins our twosome. "Good to meet you again, Stella," he adds.

"Oh, gosh. Nice to see you again, too."

My rescuer is one of the group who met our coach when it arrived in Ingelow's lovely market square. He carried my suitcase across to the hotel. In response, I've forgotten his name.

"Alex," he says, with a grin. He has a charming smile. A nice face, too; unlike my captor, who, for some reason I can't fathom, made me think of a warthog. "Settled in?"

"Yes."

"And you've had a walk round the town? You should. Be a bit careful, though. The centre is lovely, but there are some rough bits just beyond it. A dark heart beneath a smiling exterior, that's Ingelow. Wouldn't you agree, George? George? Oh dear. I seem to have driven him away. I'm terribly sorry."

"No need to apologise. He was rather a bore, actually."

Oh, God, what have I said?

Alex smiles. "He's a decent fiddle player, but he does rather go on about church architecture. Can I get you a refill?"

While he heads off to the drinks table, I study a poster hanging nearby. The Ingelow Festival presents Bach's *Mass in B minor*. The Ingleside Singers. The Fenland Orchestra (leader, Alex Collings).

"Is that you?" I ask, when he gets back.

"It is, actually. Cheers." He raises his glass and I do the same. They chink, and I hold mine up to a light and watch the little bubbles of nothingness appear from nowhere then jiggle joyfully up to the surface.

*

Morning rehearsal. My head is not at its best. Nor is the orchestra, perhaps because its leader is missing.

Alex and I had several glasses of fizz together after our first one: he was delightful company, full of stories about other concerts and (moderately) famous musicians who have visited the town in the past. Too many glasses? So many that he's wrapped his car round a tree and died in slow agony *and it's all my fault!*

Bobby says I do this – jump to 'irrationally excessive conclusions'. Concentrate on your singing, Stella.

"*Kyr* – oops, sorry. Bar too early!"

Actually, we're *all* rubbish, not just me. Even sight-reading Miranda, whom I noticed enjoyed the Champagne last night, too. Roll on lunchtime.

Roll? We get bread, curly white bread with marg and paste made out of some low form of aquatic life. I wander outside, watch the citizens of Ingelow going about their Saturday afternoon business and envy them: they're not in the middle of reducing a transcendentally gorgeous piece of music to something ear-wracking.

"Back to work, people." It's Laurence. "*Confutandis Maledictis*, from the top!"

That's the section where I mess up the most. Oh, well, it's only a weekend… I hope Bobby is having more fun trying to get a little white ball into a hole with a silly flag in it.

Alex has arrived, and is tuning up.

I want to rush over and give him a hug and say how pleased I am that he didn't die in a horrendous car accident last night. But that might seem a bit odd.

The strings re-tune to him. When they are ready, he nods to Laurence, who counts us in. The orchestra sounds ten times better already. This in turn lifts the singing. This morning's *Requiem* was a fatally wounded eagle that had been desperately flapping its wings in a failed attempt to take off, while jackals slowly circled round it. Now it is winged, airborne and has found a thermal that is sending it soaring skywards with its natural, genius-given majesty.

When the rehearsal is over, I hang around, hoping to

speak to Alex again. I'm not sure what I want to say – nothing about cars and trees – but he seemed good at creating conversation so maybe my lack of ability in that department won't matter. But he's talking to Laurence. I tag along with a group of fellow Songbirds heading back to the hotel. Probably best: I need go get myself mentally prepared for tonight.

It will be special, I tell myself.

Taking a Chance

It is.

Wolfgang Amadeus Mozart and the Sydenham Songbirds, ably assisted by the Fenland Orchestra and four soloists whose names I never quite got hold of, have done it again! Applause is ringing round the rafters of this magnificent building (magnificent, despite its Victorian glass and whatever was mediocre about its apse and its rood screen). Laurence takes yet another bow, then turns and gestures to us a third time.

Transcendent!

"I'm off to the pub," says one of the basses, as the applause begins to die down and the audience starts getting up from the rather uncomfortable pews where they have been sitting. "There's one round the corner. Anyone coming?"

"Sounds good," says Gloria. "Stella?"

"Yes. I'll… be along in a minute." I stand and tinker with my folder, still reeling with the elation of having co-created something so completely beautiful, then turn to watch Alex packing away.

I summon up courage and walk over to him.

"Hi…"

"Oh, hello, Stella. Didn't we do well?"

We. The orchestra leader talking to one rather unmusical member of the choir. "Yes!"

"Some of us are going for a drink," he goes on. "The Bakers' Arms. You get a better pint there than that God-awful plastic place round the corner. Want to join us?"

*

'Us' turns out to be just Alex, me and a group of brass players who are soon involved in a drinking contest. We find a more discreet alcove. Alex tells me about his time as a music student, playing in a provincial orchestra for a bit, how he now earns a living from teaching. "Private pupils, plus a couple of days a week at King Ethelred's – that's the posh school in town. Not that anything's really posh in Ingelow." He pauses. "But I've done far too much of the talking. You're a very good listener, but I want to hear about you, too. Tell me about Stella."

"I'm a Philosopher," I say.

No, I do. Honestly. Where the hell did that come from?

Alex breaks into a broad smile.

"Well, I did it at uni," I add hastily. "Polytechnic, actually."

He doesn't seem concerned about the grade of my educational establishment. "I regard myself as a philosopher, too. Are you familiar with Nietzsche's *The Birth of Tragedy from the Spirit of Music*?"

"Familiar? I loved it!" I say, then try desperately to remember what it was about. "Apollo and Dionysus… The… union of pure classical beauty and the energy of the life force."

"Exactly! The Artist, especially the Composer, as a priest of the transcendent in a vulgar world!"

"The reconnection of alienated of humanity to its natural emotional and spiritual roots!" I add, because suddenly I am back in a cramped little room that smells of old books; me and the other five members of The Enlightenment Club, listening to the words of Dr Stanislas Licht.

A jukebox in one corner, which has been silent up till

now, begins to play *Take a Chance on Me.*

Alex grimaces. "God, I wish they hadn't installed that thing. Especially when it plays bloody Abba. God, I hate Abba! I write proper music. I'm working on a concerto. I have been for a while – the birth pangs are proving hard on this one. Would you like to hear it? As far as I've got, anyway."

"I'd love to."

"Come on. Drink up."

As we get up to leave, the brass players give a raucous cheer, presumably something to do with their drinking game.

*

The church door creaks open. Alex finds the lights: the sound of the switches booms round the nave, as do our footsteps and the plop of him putting his violin case down on a pew. He gets out the instrument – there is such delicacy in how he holds it and nestles it under his chin.

"May I present the first movement of the violin concerto in E, by Alex Collings!"

La, laaaaaa, la, la, laaaaaaaa. Da, da, da, da, da, da.

The door creaks again. "Hello?" calls out a voice.

"Fuck," says Alex. The word also echoes round the nave.

"Oh, Mr Collings, it's you."

"Yes, Joe."

"I thought you lot had all gone. I've got to lock the church up now."

"Can we have another ten minutes?"

"Sorry. It's later than the vicar agreed anyway."

"Ten minutes. This is important."

"Locked up at ten o'clock, Mr Johnstone said."

"Bloody philistine," Alex mutters. A look of sudden, intense fury crosses his face. Then he seems to rein it in;

maybe it's putting the violin back in its lining that has this calming effect. He even smiles. How admirable, I think. Philosophical, above petty annoyances… "We could go back to my place and I'll play it for you there, if you like," he says.

*

There's a grand piano in the middle of Alex's big, main room. The walls are covered with more posters of concerts. There are bookshelves, way more than we have back home, laden like the ones – once revived, the memory of The Enlightenment Club is crystal-clear, now – in the Doctor's old study.

Alex gets out the violin with his usual affection, tunes up – then suggests we have a drink first. Glass of wine? Well, why not? We sit on a big sinky sofa and talk.

"You're a real inspiration, Stella."

"That's very kind of you."

"No, I mean it. You make me feel… free, somehow. To create. To make art. To take on all that bad stuff. Laziness. Mediocrity. Inauthenticity. Nietzsche understood this so well. If we aren't true to ourselves, who can we be true to?"

"No…"

He sighs. "I've spent so much of my life living half truthfully, Stella. I've not totally given in, but… I know I can do better."

I point to the posters. "You've done better than most people."

"So?" He shakes his head. "Most people sit in pubs and listen to Abba on jukeboxes. I want more, Stella. I want 'true'. Beautiful. Inspired. Those satisfactions come from Great Art, and nothing else…" He pauses. A frown crosses his face, just briefly, then he cheers up. "Your glass is empty. Have some

85

more!"

Various voices tell me to refuse.

"Thank you," I say.

The wine makes a lovely glugging sound. I suddenly feel I belong here, with the piano, the posters of concerts, the books, doing whatever I can to help this beautiful man make Great Art.

Right

"Anyone at home?"

"Yes. Hello Bobby!"

"Had a good time?"

"Yes. We were fantastic, and the audience loved it!"

"Good." The clubs clank as he puts them next to the elephant's foot umbrella-stand.

"Good rounds?" I ask.

"Oh, the usual ups and downs. I played a great shot at the 14th on Saturday. Must have been a hundred and fifty yards and ended up three feet from the hole. Then I missed the putt. Drive for show, putt for dough, as they say. Crazy game!"

"Maybe I ought to learn, so we could play together."

"If you don't mind being driven mad."

"I'm mad already," I say flippantly, then cross over to him and put my arms round him. He is a little surprised and makes a gesture halfway between a squeeze and a flinch.

"It's nice to see you," I say, feeling an explanation for my action is needed. "Fancy a tea?"

I go into the kitchen and turn on the kettle: silent at first, it begins to gurgle, then to jiggle about with a kind of insane, dancer's joy, belching steam. Then it gives a click and falls silent.

As I plop the bags into two mugs (*Plastex '87, Milwaukee* and *Plastex '89, Stuttgart*), I tell myself that the best thing to do is to be upfront and tell him now.

Everything.

I take the tea through. "There's something…"

Bobby looks up at me, detecting the seriousness in my voice.

"…wonderful about a cup of tea after a long journey, isn't there?" I go on.

*

I ought to tell *you* what happened, though, shouldn't I?

We drank a toast to Art, and talked more about music – well, he did most of the talking – and then he suddenly broke off and looked terribly sad. "I've not lived up to my dreams," he said, and I told him, "Not yet." Then he took me by the hand and said how badly he needed inspiration, and I was the sort of special person who could provide it.

I knew two things as he said that; one that I should terminate the conversation at once, and two that it was completely impossible for me to do so. Instead, I felt myself leaning forward to plant a kiss on his cheek. It felt so nice under my lips that I did it again, consciously, this time. My choice. We moved our lips to each other's, and it felt so good and right and my due…

Of course, I'm not proud of that, and even less proud about what happened afterwards. But I felt such longing at that moment, of a kind I had never felt before. It wasn't just about physical desire, though there was plenty of that, years and years of it. This was spiritual and aesthetic, philosophical. This was about Philosophy and Great Art.

*

On the train in to work, I rootle in my bag and find the card he gave me.

Alex Collings
Musician, Composer
26 Common Road

Cawston
Ingelow
AT29 8QX

When I get to Blackfriars, I'll find a bin and drop it in there. That night was wonderful, but now it's back to real life. I've got my memories, of feeling beautiful in a place dedicated to beauty.

When I get there, I can't find a bin.

At work, I wait till nobody else is around, then take the card out again.

Alex Collings
Musician, Composer
26 Common Road
Cawston
Ingelow
AT29 8QX

There's a bin here, but people might look in it and ask questions. I'll find some other way of getting rid of it.

Tomorrow.

Maybe.

*

I become two people.

Old Stella is unaffected by the trip to Ingelow and gets on with things exactly as before.

New Stella is bright-hearted and young again – no, young for the first time, as when she was actually young, she was always struggling (except for ten evenings in a tiny room full of books and tapes and Philosophy and the music of Wolfgang Amadeus Mozart). New Stella is ambitious again. New Stella buys books, even if there's no space for them, and puts on Radio Three when she's doing the washing up (though still switches off if the piece is too – what's the word? – lacking in melody). New Stella is in love.

'Where are you taking me?' Old asks New.

'To my true self,' New answers back.

'I don't know what you're talking about!'

'No, you don't, do you?'

A third Stella, Sensible, moderate, come-on-everyone-let's-sort-this-out Stella, tries to mediate.

You've already got so much in your life, she tells New Stella. Be grateful for that.

'I need more!' New Stella snaps back.

*

One evening, Bobby's out at a Chamber of Commerce meeting and all the Stellas are sitting at home, reading their new book on existentialism. Human beings define themselves through action, the book says.

So do something!

A letter would be best. Things can go wrong on telephones. I get out our smart, light blue Basildon Bond writing paper, and even the act of doing so, and selecting a pen, and putting it on the soft surface of the paper, seems daring and venturesome. And when I write *Dear Alex...*

'This is wrong!' says Old Stella. 'Stop!'

I do not stop.

No big declaration. Just a meeting. Even sensible, moderate, come-on-everyone-let's-sort-this-out Stella has to admit that anything is better than the current impasse. Seeing Alex again might solve the whole thing. He'll suddenly look ridiculously pretentious and provincial, or he'll let slip some unpleasant thing about his past – he hasn't told me a lot about his emotional history – and suddenly this infatuation (all of us

Stellas know that's what this really is) will be over.

New Stella scribbles *that* address on the matching light blue envelope and heads off to the postbox, where she balances the letter on the lip of the slot then flips it in, with the kind of flip an existentialist Philosopher would give when posting a letter to one of her many passionate and exotic lovers, before heading off to the café where Jean-Paul and Simone and maybe Albert, back from Algeria, are waiting.

Old Stella watches, helpless.

*

One o'clock, we said, didn't we? I treble-check the name of the restaurant I had suggested, a quiet, discreet one in town I used to go to with Malcolm (not the posh one), then look up at its clock again.

He's not coming.

I stare into the glass of fizzy water that I ordered. The bubbles appear, make their brief journey to the top then pop.

'This is for the best,' says Old Stella.

'Yes,' says moderator Stella, kindness in her voice. 'It's time to move on.'

New Stella stays in her seat and keeps staring at the bubbles.

Customers arrive and settle in. Couples smile at each other and enjoy debating the items on the menu. I feel a sudden rage…

"Stella!"

"Alex!"

"I'm sorry. The train…"

"That's fine," I say, the rage dissipated in an instant. He looks even handsomer than he did in Ingelow. He stretches out his hand – an Artist's hand, strong but gentle, formed by the creation of Cartesian points of beauty. I hold out my accountant/office manager's hand and he takes it anyway, then steps closer and makes to put his artist's arms around me. I back off, then feel ashamed of this bashfulness and let him hug me. Then we kiss on the cheek and retreat to our places across the table.

'You're supposed to be finding reasons not to like him,' Old Stella reminds me.

"So – how's the music?" I begin.

"I'm still a bit stuck with the concerto, but… I've been doing a lot more playing since you got back in touch." He gives one of his smiles.

"That's… great."

"We're doing a concert in a couple of months. Nothing adventurous, I'm afraid. I'd love you to come and listen. You're always welcome to stay over," he adds.

The waiter reappears. "What would madam like?"

To go to Alex's concert and stay over. "Vegetable lasagna, please."

"Would madam like wine?"

"No, I'd – better not."

"Have half a glass, at least," says Alex.

"Well, OK then. But that's all."

*

"Shall I order another bottle?"

"No, I must do *some* work this afternoon."

"Coffee, though?"

"Oh, yes."

Coffee means another quarter of an hour of music, philosophy, Apollo, Dion – whatever he's called… But of course, it ends, as it has to. Alex insists on paying the bill, leaves a generous tip, and we walk slowly towards the tube station.

"So…" he says.

"It's… difficult," I reply.

"Life's difficult. That is why Art is."

Because Art is difficult, we share a proper kiss by the great big Underground symbol. Then I really have to go. I trudge back to work, but in my heart I am on the tube, then on the 15.25 to Ingelow, and then on the road back to Cawston and 26 Common Road and that sofa and…

Holy Matrimony is not by any to be enterprised nor taken in hand unadvisedly, lightly or wantonly, but reverently, discreetly, advisedly, soberly.

What am I doing?

*

When Bobby comes back that evening, I hold him for a long, long time.

"Are you OK?" he asks.

"Yes… I'm fine." He doesn't look convinced. "Bad day at work," I add.

"Smells like you had rather a good day."

"Oh, yes, well – that was the problem. A couple of the girls and I went out and had a bottle of wine, and Trevor got all ratty about it."

"I can see his point of view. Productivity losses due to excessively long lunches cost the economy billions of… Ah, but everyone needs to celebrate from time to time. Any special reason?"

"One of the temps was leaving." The lie is odious – aren't I trying to be more truthful? – but telling it is terrifyingly easy.

We talk idly over the dinner, then Bobby says he's turning in early. He's got 'a bit of a day' tomorrow.

"I'll join you," I say cheerfully.

"Good idea," he says, though he doesn't sound hugely excited. In bed, he gives me a peck, rolls over and nods off, leaving me alone with my thoughts. *Reverently, discreetly, advisedly, soberly*, I remind myself.

Then suddenly Alex and I are on that sofa.

Di-es illa!

*

I wander downstairs next morning and pick up the *Times* from the doormat. I wonder what Alex reads. The *Guardian* probably. Or maybe he despises all media for their inauthenticity. I make a mug of tea – *Plastex '86, Chicago* – and curl up on the sofa, cradling the drink in my hands. Bobby appears a few minutes later. At the same moment, post clanks in through the letterbox. Bobby wanders over to it, as if he expected its arrival to coincide with his, and begins sorting through it.

"I can't stand it any longer!" I exclaim suddenly.

"I know. The amount of junk mail one gets these days."

"No I mean my life. Our life. Here…"

"Oh. What's wrong?"

"I don't know," I lie, suddenly horrified at my outburst. Is there a time machine I could borrow, so I could pop back thirty seconds? That's all I'd need…

"Hmph!" says Bobby. "That's… Can we talk about this later? I've got… Have a think, Stella. Get some things down on paper. A list we can go through and sort out."

"A list?"

"First step in problem-solving: specify the issues. If you

draw up a list, we can sort it all out." He gives me an optimistic grin.

*

"Done that list?" he says that evening.

"No."

"Oh. Why not?"

"I don't know," I say, ashamed to admit that I've got through half a notepad, then, an hour ago, started flushing the scrunched up bits of paper down the loo, realized that would soon block it, taken the rest of them into the garden and, after triple-checking that nobody was looking, set light to them, then cleared up the ashes with a dustpan and brush and mixed them in with other stuff in the black dustbin. Even this, I know, isn't perfect: I've seen things on the TV where the police can take charred paper and find out what was on them.

"Stella, you've got to be more proactive."

"I… know."

"So what's the problem?"

"I… need to be myself."

"Oh… But… you are yourself, aren't you? Who else could you be?"

"I don't know. Nobody?"

"That doesn't make sense. Everybody's somebody. Nobody's nobody. Well, I suppose that's obvious really." He pauses. "I don't really understand this 'being yourself' stuff. We're just… who we are. Aren't we? I'm me; you're you… I really think you need to make a list. Come up with some specific action points."

Silence falls.

This is, of course, ridiculous.

"Bobby, I've met someone else."

He stares at me for what seems like forever, then turns away. I stare, too, at the back of his head, appalled at what I've just said but at the same time overcome with a terrible relief. I want him to swing round and erupt with fury, the alpha male furiously defending what is his.

He turns round slowly. "Oh," he says.

Silence again.

"He's called Alex Collings," I blurt out. "He's a musician. He's…" Then I can't think of anything to say.

"I'm not very musical, am I?"

"No. But it's not just that."

"Oh. What is it, then? No, don't say. I don't want to know." Another long pause. "We'd better *both* do a list, Stella."

*

- I'll write to Alex, wishing him well but saying I shan't be in touch again.
- Bobby and I will talk more.
- We will make love at least once a week.
- I'll give up the choir.

(Bobby recommended using bullet points.)

Well, what else can I do? Marriage made me an adult. Am I going to be a teenager again? God help me, no way!

"God is dead," mutters a Germanic-sounding voice in my head.

*

I hoped the pain would abate. The boil lanced, a natural healing process would then take over. That's what it's like for adults, isn't it?

It gets worse.

Several months later, I'm walking past the old Poly. Huge

articulated lorries are, as usual, thundering by, like predatory dinosaurs, a few feet from my face, on their way to Dover and the world beyond.

'Go on,' says a voice in my head.

Go on what?

'You know you want to.'

Want to what?

'Finish the whole bloody charade. Here's God knows how many tons of metal travelling way in excess of 30 mph. Just step out in front of the next one, and the pretence will be all over.'

No!

'Yes! Authenticity, that's what life is for. If you can't live truthfully, you're just a fake, a non-person, nothing, a phoney, a coward. *Salaud*, that's what Sartre would call you.'

Huh! It's all right for him. He was a writer. He was a professional Philosopher. He was French. I'm an accountant/office-manager from South London.

The next tyrannosaur barrels past.

Salaud!

Carlo's Café has been replaced by a trendy bistrot (I stopped going to Carlo's ages ago, and one day it was just boarded up; I never even got to say goodbye to Carlo). I hurry in and find the remotest seat, where I order a mug of lightly-scented hot water, alias 'bergamot and mandarin tzigane'. It costs as much as a full plate of bangers, eggs and chips plus unlimited refills of dark brown tea did in the old days.

"I'm doing what's right," I tell myself. "Right!"

People turn and give me funny looks. They do not understand. Another monster rumbles by and makes tiny ripples in the soulless water.

'The bitter tears begin to flow.'

The manager comes over and asks me to leave, as I am disturbing the other customers.

*

I call Lucy, and arrange to stay at hers for a bit. Then I go back to the house and pack. What things do I want? Very few.

I leave a note.

Everything you do is by the rules… Philosophy and Great Art mean nothing to you… Despite your ridiculous 'list', things haven't changed because you can't change.

I write it, re-read it (several times), edit it a bit – put in a bit more venom! – Oh, no, that was way below the belt – then think it's horrible and shove it down the sink disposal unit, which takes ages to chew it up. Clearly the unit finds self-serving cruelty indigestible.

I write another note. *I'm just going away for a few days… Nothing to worry about…*

The sink unit dislikes lies, too.

I get writing again.

Dear Bobby,

This is written in great turmoil and great sadness. I've tried desperately to make things work, but over the last months I have felt more and more a stranger in our own home, in my own self, even. I can't stand it any longer, and don't know what to do other than leave.

You are a decent man, and deserve better than this: the fault is all mine, but in the end, that doesn't change things. I wish it did.

It would be wrong of me to string you along, saying that 'one day I might come back'. I don't know what the future holds, but I must set out without promises I cannot guarantee to keep.

You have things to support you that I do not have – friends (it's true, all 'our' friends, not that we see them often, are his), *your work, a faith* (do I have one? Not any longer). *These are deserved – you are a better person than I am. I beg you to use them and find real happiness.*

I am so terribly sorry about this.
    With affection and enormous regret
        Stella

I consider putting this down the unit too, just to see what it thinks of this version. But I must trust my own judgement. I add a PS, that I'm going to Lucy's for a bit, then reread the note. Maybe I should take out that line about –

No.

Just go.

Wonderful

A mechanical female voice reads off the list of the remaining stations (I imagine her as a cartoon robot with a blonde wig on). Little Groaning, Podsworth, Ingelow.

I look round at my fellow passengers (the train got a lot emptier after Cambridge) and wonder if any of them are making life-changing journeys, too. They all look rather bored.

It already feels a lifetime ago that I left Bobby. Lucy has been bloody marvellous, listening to me talk, talk, talk and only occasionally telling me I should have done this years ago. She also said that I should contact Alex a.s.a.b.p. However, some sense of propriety stopped me. Just rushing off into the arms of someone else seemed vulgar. Lucy shrugged when I said this, and asked me how long I wanted to punish myself.

Bobby and I talked, of course. His moods varied, and I wished with all my heart that the hurt ones would go away, but I know they wouldn't and they won't for a long while. I'm suddenly grateful to those dinos on the South Circular: reminders of why there is no going back.

"I expect you'll be after me for half of everything," he said at one point, and I replied no, I hated the thought of him being turfed out of his home or losing control of the company. "All I want is to be me," I said.

This seemed to annoy him more than if I'd insisted on hiring the most expensive divorce lawyers. "What the fuck do you mean by that?"

"I'll… tell you when I find out," I reply.

One evening, MC Lucy-fer (that's her new incarnation) is out doing a gig. I sit and stare at the phone, then begin dialing that number I know by heart…

Now here I am, invited for the weekend.

The robot – for some reason, I've named her Caroline – informs me that our final 'station stop' will be Ingelow. The train begins to slow down. Caroline reminds me to take all my luggage with me. Then we are here! The doors whoosh open. I gather my things – in my mind, I see Caroline giving a forced grin of approval – and step out. The wind is salt-sharp and invigorating.

Alex is standing at the other end of the platform. He breaks into a huge grin as he spots me; I break into a run. When we meet, there's a moment when we just look at each other, then we are in each other's arms. We kiss, tentatively at first, then I clamp my lips over his and wait for him to shove his tongue into my mouth, which he does, a little slower than I'd like, but with, once it happens, real conviction. I feel myself jolt to life (just as Caroline must have, when her creator first attached the electrodes).

When we stop, the platform is empty.

He takes my case in one hand – it's not heavy; I'm travelling without baggage in every way. With his other hand, he takes mine in a firm grip, and we walk out to his car. Inside, we share another ravenous kiss, then drive off, past plain brick houses and take-aways, which are probably rubbish but which suddenly look hauntingly exotic. We don't say much. We don't need to. Soon we're out in the flat-looking countryside, then in a village, then crunching across gravel.

I want him to pick me up and carry me over the threshold, but he fiddles with the front door key then does a kind of ushering-me-in gesture. "Do you want a coffee or something?" he asks.

"I want to make love with you," I say.

*

He has a small bottle of Champagne in the bedside cabinet, which we drink sitting up in bed. I hold my glass to the light of the window and do my bubble-watching thing, though I now know the bubbles are joyous things. If you must have a short existence that ends with a pop, then do so exuberantly, with passion! I want to tell my lover how utterly wonderful it felt doing what we have just done, but I can't find the words. Maybe a piece of music would do the job better. *Lux aeterna?*

So we just drink, then touch each other again, then simultaneously decide to get up and wander back down to the big main room, where I sink into the sofa and stare at the fireplace by which we are going to spend long evenings talking Music and Philosophy and the Nature of Art, and every now and then make love (with the *Dies Irae* on the stereo at full volume? OK, it's a bit short: maybe it could be on a loop…)

Alex rustles up a meal: at one point I pad across the floor – earthy old flagstones, covered in places by an assortment of rugs – to see if he needs help. He gives me a squeeze and says it's nearly ready: I get some plates out then just sit and look at him doling out pasta and supermarket meat sauce and know this is going to be the most delicious meal I've ever tasted. After it, we snuggle on the sofa. A furry black cat, which Alex introduces as Liszt (Brahms, he tells me, got run over a couple of years back), appears and settles onto my lap.

"Now!" he says suddenly. "Now's the time for me to play you my concerto."

"Yes, please!"

"It's not actually finished – but I've made progress. I did

102

some writing today that felt really good."

"Brilliant."

The fiddle is sitting on the piano. He picks it up, with such love, and tunes it.

"Right," he says. "Music for my Muse."

La, laaaaaa, la, la, laaaaaaaa. Da, da, da, da, da, da…

The cat screeches, digs his claws into my thighs and flees into the kitchen.

Alex stops. "Damn. Sorry about that. Start again…" He tucks the violin under his chin, raises the bow, then shakes his head. "The moment… It's gone. I'll play it tomorrow."

He starts putting the fiddle into its case, then pauses. We both have the same idea at the same time. "Here, hold it," he says.

The violin is lighter than I expected. It feels extraordinarily delicate, but also powerful and alive. It is the Spirit of Art.

"Bach!" Alex exclaims. "We should listen to Bach."

We do, then it's bed again. Our lovemaking is inspired by the music we have just heard; it is slow, intricate, deep. Then cuddles and sleep – for Alex, anyway. I lie awake, wondering what I have done to deserve this. I run my hands over his face and chest, then lie back listening to his slow, steady breathing.

Find one point of absolute certainty, then build on it.

*

Next morning, Alex says he should really rehearse the concerto before playing it to me. I say that's fine; I'll have a wander round the village. Cawston smells of the sea. It has low cottages made from reddish-brown stone, a green (or at least a triangle of grass), a pub (the Crusoe Arms), and a church made of flints. I hesitate at the gate of the churchyard

– is it really authentic for a Nietzschean to go in and have a nose?

A Nietzschean can go anywhere, do anything!

The church turns out to be locked. As I walk back down the path, I read the names on the graves and wonder which of these people found true love in their lives and which of them had to make do with second best.

When I get back, the concerto is still not quite ready. No problem. Alex plays me some stuff on the piano, then it's time for the Crusoe Arms. We get drunk, which is delicious.

"To art and alcohol!" says Alex, raising his final glass. "The two things that make life worth living!"

"And love," I add.

He grins. "Yes, of course. And love!" He looks me in the eye, winks and we clink glasses.

On Sunday morning… I'd rather not go into that. Alex is, let's say, adventurous sexually. Of course! He's an Artist!

In the afternoon we go for a long walk on Ingelow North Beach, which is only a couple of miles away. There are gaggles of tourists for bit, then just sand, shells, wind, clumps of bladderwrack, the occasional gull – and me and my Creator of Beauty. And the sea itself, of course, still distant. Alex says that when the tide comes in it's so fast that walkers can be outpaced by it. People have drowned here: their own stupid fault, of course, but one needs to be careful.

I glance out at the thin white line on the horizon and will it to come roaring in, as I have an affinity with everything wild and powerful.

Terrible

I head back to London very early Monday morning, on a special train for zombies, but it seems pointless being there. Ingelow is where I have to be.

I hand in my notice at Happy Daze. They say I can leave at the end of the week: I feel a little insulted but also delighted.

So at the end of that week I'm heading up to my new home town and checking into a B and B on London Road. It's spartan but it's cheap. It's only going to be temporary, I know. I get a copy of the Ingelow Trumpet on Saturday morning, and by mid-afternoon Monday I have a job as accountant/office-manager for Zzapp! Marketing (I tell myself I'll find something more suitable for the Muse of an Artist later), starting straight away.

"We have a Positive Attitude here," says Stuart, my new boss, as he shows me into my office.

"Suits me," I reply.

"Your Thoughts make you who you are," he continues. "Think Positive, Be Positive."

"That's me!" says victorious New Stella.

I spend a lot of time at Alex's, and find myself doing more and more about this music-filled house. Lucy would give me a lecture at this point about giving in to the patriarchy, but the place is a bit of a mess, I feel good sorting that out and Alex appreciates it. Stuart would call that a Win/Win Outcome. Soon, it makes obvious sense that I move in. When I suggest it, Alex is not as delighted as I hoped he'd be, but he sees the logic of it.

"We Philosophers are logical," I say.

Nietzsche, he points out, disliked logic, and we have a little debate about that. Dr Licht always said that Nietzsche was fiercely logical in his own way. Alex says that for him, one of the joys of Nietzsche was his dethronement of logic and its replacement with Art as the central human experience.

We're saying the same thing, really, but just in slightly different ways.

I still haven't heard the concerto. After a brief burst of creativity, Alex got stuck again, and he really wants to wait till it's ready. I wonder what Muse-like things I can do to help him along. Mozart needed no encouragement from Constanze: his art just flowed. Nietzsche? Did he need the odd prod about getting on with *Also Sprach Zarathustra*? Come on, Friedrich – or did she call him Fred? Freddie? Walrus-face? – you've been staring at that page all morning!

Just be yourself, Stella.

We both want to make music together: he'll play piano; I'll sing. Alex suggests Schubert's *An die muzik*.

I need a little time to familiarize myself with it. This means waiting till nobody's about, then sitting at the keyboard and picking out the melody note by note – why couldn't Schubert write the bloody thing in C? Liszt watches me as I do this, and I make him promise not to tell Alex quite how poor my sight-reading is. In return, I give him a sachet of beef in jelly rather than the usual dried stuff. Then I discover that Alex has a recording (he might have told me!) I play it and hear something so different to what I have been coming up with that I have to check it's the same piece.

Oh, well, as Stuart says, it's not the start that matters, but how you finish. We perform it one evening; I think I do rather well, but Alex says it 'needs quite a lot of work'.

We don't do much work on it, however, as he has a new project that seems to take up all his spare energy: a quartet to play twentieth-century chamber music. I ask if they need a 'roadie' and tell him about Lucy and the band, but he grimaces and says they are not a pop group.

They organize a performance – Alex doesn't like the word 'gig' – at St Jude's. They practise hard, especially the Schönberg, usually round at ours. It's not really my kind of music, but I'm happy to do stuff in the kitchen, bring in occasional cups of tea, and console the cat, who is obviously scared of visitors.

The performance takes place. Hardly anyone turns up. I guess the venue isn't ideal: those seats aren't very comfy. But I can't help feeling the choice of music plays a part. I think of when we filled this place with the soaring harmonies of Wolfgang Amadeus Mozart – and with happy, uplifted people. I remind myself how Alex made that all happen, how dreadful the orchestra was until he came along and breathed life into it.

Afterwards we go to the pub. Alex gets the first round, or rather pays for it out of the takings at the door, after which there is £5.43 left.

"This town's full of bloody philistines," he mutters as he slams down the tray.

"Come on, Alex," says David, the viola player. "Contemporary music is a minority taste, but so what? As long as the folk who turned up enjoyed it, then we've done a good job."

"You get more people at a village football match than we did," Alex says. "What does it say about the sort of world we live in?"

"You should let me help with the publicity next time," I suggest.

Walter, the double bass player, mumbles a comment into his bushy beard. I'm not sure I've ever made out a word he's said, but Alex nods energetically. "Too damn right, Walter. All the 'publicity' in the world won't change how fucking pig-ignorant most people are. Jesus Christ…"

He says the word 'publicity' with a real sneer. The poor turnout has really hurt, I can tell.

*

Next evening, it's Alex's 'proper' pub night. I like drinking with him, but I can't keep up: it's best once a week that he has a free hand.

I sit at home and watch TV, then suddenly, for the first time since coming here, I feel alone. I don't know why; it just suddenly hits me. I need to talk to someone.

I've not spoken to Lucy for a while. I know that's horribly ungrateful after the help she gave me, but this is *my* adventure, *my* life-changing experience, and Lucy does have a way of muscling in on things. But the moment I hear her voice – all jangly and Catford for the first few sentences then gently drifting back to her natural Sydenham – I realize how much I've missed her.

She tells me about a big gig coming up next week, in a field somewhere in Oxfordshire. And about her new man.

"He owns a record company!" she says.

"I thought you hated record companies," I reply.

"Yes, well, that was when nobody would sign us. Weekend after next, we're off to LA."

"Los Angeles?"

"Yes, Stella. Los Angeles."

"Well, I thought you despised Los Angeles. 'The place where capitalism is at its most evil,' you once called it. 'Where it apes art and leaches its venom into the creative heart of a once freedom-loving nation,' you once called it."

"Well remembered, Stells. We'll only be there a month." She pauses. "Zavvy's not what you think, Stells. He's…" She pauses again. "Nice. Everything still wonderful for you?"

"Of course!" I reply. As I say that, I realize that's a lie, and that I'm phoning because the precise opposite is true. But I don't want to say that. I can't say that.

"Maybe we've both cracked it at the same time," Lucy says chirpily. "We could have some kind of joint ceremony!"

"Ceremony?"

"Yes. Why not? If we've both found The One… I've always rather fancied a handfasting on top of a mountain."

"Maybe." I'm not sure what handfasting is, but I sense Alex would not like it. And there is a distinct lack of mountains around Ingelow, anyway.

We talk a bit more, then she has to get ready, as Zavvy is taking her to some restaurant I've never heard of but apparently should have.

When I put the receiver down, I want to feel I have osmosed a little of my sister's happiness. But if I have, it soon leaks away. I seek out my old phone book. Almost everyone in it is either a friend of Bobby's or someone I've lost touch with years ago.

Vee is now Mrs Jenkinson.

"Oh hello…" Pause. "How are you, Stella?"

"I'm OK."

"Good." Another pause. "You gave us all a shock."

"Oh. Do you think ill of me?"

"You're a friend."

"But if I wasn't?"

"That's a hypothetical question."

"People have to be true to themselves, you know."

"Even if it hurts other people?"

"Nietzsche said…" I begin, then run out of inspiration. "I suppose, sometimes, yes."

There's a brief silence. "How's the family?" I ask.

*

Alex gets back particularly late. I'm in bed, and I hear him clumping around the kitchen. I want him to come upstairs and be with me, but the clumping continues; I pull on my dressing gown and make my way down to where he's staring at the empty fireplace.

"Good evening?" I ask cheerily.

"No."

"Oh, er… What happened?"

"I did."

I don't understand what he means, but I put my arms round him anyway. He tries to push me away, then pulls me to him. We sit there for quite a while, then he lets out a loud belch.

"Overdone it," he says, getting unsteadily to his feet and wandering off to the kitchen. He reappears holding a glass of water. "I guess I'd better sleep down here tonight."

"No. You don't have to. I like it when you sleep beside me."

He turns to me and fixes me with a scowl I've not seen before. "I'm a such a bloody fool."

"What's happened?" I ask again.

"Nietzsche was right. The Artist is a priest. A priest of

110

the trans – trans – a priest of the sublime in a vulgar, sell-out world. God is dead; long live music. Proper music, serious music, that is. Not fucking Abba or even Classics For fucking Pleasure."

"Absolutely!" I say, though a little bit of me thinks at once what's wrong with Classics for Pleasure? Would he prefer Classics for Misery?'

Maybe he senses this. He looks me in the eye. "No, Stella. You don't believe that. At all. That's the problem. You believe in the way someone 'believes' who turns up at church on Christmas day, sings a couple of carols and comes away thinking how spiritual they are. That's not priesthood. Priesthood means sacrifice, dedication, sublib… blob…"

I never find out what else priesthood means, as he spills his water all over his trousers. "Oh, fuck it! *Fuck it!*"

I'm a little scared, but suddenly angry too. I need to defend myself from those comments. But instead – I'm not proud of this, but it's what happens – I get a fit of the giggles.

"Yes, hilarious, isn't it? Father Collings has been at the Communion wine again. And he has seen the light. Again. Again! Hallelujah!"

I start stuttering out an apology, but it's no good.

"Let's talk in the morning," I say.

*

At 4.30 I'm in the kitchen making a cup of tea. Then I go into the big room, sit on the edge of a chair and stare round at the music, the books, at Alex, who slept on the sofa after all. His face has been released from last night's ugliness and looks beautiful again. Maybe you can only really know someone when they've made a complete chump of themselves in front of you. I head back up to bed and actually sleep a bit.

The alarm goes off at its usual time. I make breakfast – well, get some bowls out and put cereal in them. Alex sits down, stares into his Krispi-Flakes then at me. "This hasn't worked, has it?" he says.

"I'll do boiled eggs tomorrow if you like."

"I mean us, Stella. You and me. We live in different worlds."

"That's not true, Alex."

"It is true. You're one of those women for whom Art is a kind of plaything, a decoration, something that makes the world nicer and prettier."

I manage a defence this time, though I know "No, I'm not!" isn't exactly insightful.

"I've lived this stuff. I've lain awake at night wrestling with the pain it causes."

A different tack. "Tell me about it, then, Alex. Let me in. Let me see."

"I shouldn't have to." He sighs. "Your old teacher was right, Stella. *Be true to yourself.* I can't do that and live with you. It's as simple as that."

I try to summon a reply. None comes. I try to look him in the eye. He looks away. I stare round this room, a place I have come to associate with love and truth and Art –

"I want you to pack your stuff and leave," he says.

"Pack?"

"I can't stand long, drawn-out farewells. If something's over, it's over."

"Over?"

"Over. I'll call a taxi if you like."

"Taxi?"

"What do you want me to do, Stella?" he snaps.

"Give us… a bit more time."

"Why?"

"Because I'm in love with you," I say. "I'm not a musician of your calibre. I never was. You knew that. I just… You said… I wanted…" My voice tails away.

He starts shaking his head.

*

The landlady at the B and B helps me up the stairs with my universe.

"Good to see you back again," she says. "Give me a shout if there's anything you need."

A reason to live?

I fling myself onto the hard, lumpy bed and the tears well up. There is nothing to break their flow now, no last shreds of dignity to preserve, so that's what they do, flow, for what seems like hours.

Then, as suddenly as they started, they stop. I unpack the case: some toiletries; a few clothes; Malcolm's pottery shard (which I've kept in a box all these years. Don't ask me why. Just don't, OK?) A photo of myself with Lucy when we were girls. I arrange them on the bed. I love them so much! Then I can't stand their company a moment longer and must have fresh air.

I end up in a café near the bus station, sitting at a formica-topped table, sipping a cup of stewed tea and watching life go on all around me.

Life. Real life. Obese mums, tattooed dads, crop-haired boys with plastic toy guns, cutesy girls clutching anorexic dolls, grandparents old at 55 with rubbish teeth and stooping gaits. Lives far superior to mine, as they involve family, children, belonging.

Unexamined lives, the Philosopher in me objects.

Lives.

A baby a few tables away starts screaming, and I have to be on the move again. A shaven-headed man with a ring in his nose holds the door open for me as I hurry out, and I'm so bloody lost in myself that I don't even thank him.

This time, I find myself at the train station. One of the books Dr Licht got us reading was *Anna Karenina*.

No! I shake my head angrily. But why not get *onto* a train and head back to London?

No.

What Alex said was unkind and stupid, but people say unkind and stupid things. Better than keeping it all bottled up! When he comes round to apologise, we'll clear the air and …

Get real, Stella!

I get real. But I'm not going back to London. It would mean admitting failure to Bobby, to Lucy, to Mother, to Mr bloody Brown and his stuck-up daughter, to the Poly (or whatever it is now) which I'll probably have to creep past every morning on the way to some shitty new job. Worst of all, to myself.

I came here for a reason.

What reason?

I need to find out.

I head for the river, where I sit watching a piece of rubbish bobbing along, admiring its resilience. Then it sinks. I head back to the B and B via an off-license, where I ask for something cheap and alcoholic. The storekeeper recommends a peach brandy, which I take to my room and swig from.

It's rather nice, actually.

*

"Feeling better, Stella?" Stuart is dressed in a bird suit.

"Yes, thanks. It was just one of those 24-hour things."

"Good. Like the outfit?" The bird suit has stubby little wings and a long, orange beak that looks like a semi-erect penis and that waggles uncontrollably as its wearer speaks. "Meet Osbert the Oystercatcher. The new mascot for Ingelow Town FC. Kleep! Kleep! That's the noise oystercatchers make, by the way. I looked it up. Kleep! Kleep!"

I retreat into my office and switch on the computer. The accounts of Zzapp! Marketing immediately fill my life with order and meaning – for about five minutes, then I find myself in tears again.

Several hankies later, the crying stops. When I'm sure my eyes aren't red any longer, I head for the coffee machine. Company, that's what I need.

Millie, one of the designers, is there. "Hi Stella. How's it going?"

"Fine!" I reply.

"Cool!" she says, taking her mug and heading off.

To receive consolation, one must first admit loss. I hover by the machine, waiting for someone to appear. No-one does. The phone rings, which I'm supposed to answer. Someone else gets it. I hover on. *I need consolation.*

"Hello Stella." It's Richard, our IT expert.

"Hi."

"You don't look happy. What's up?"

Out with it! "My partner and I have split up."

"Bad luck." He takes a milk carton and sniffs it cautiously. "Some life-forms reproduce asexually. Sea-squirts, for example. I often think that is a superior strategy. Do you think this milk is OK?"

I take the coffee back to my office and finish it. It is, as usual, revolting. But maybe it's all I'm worth.

"You OK?" Deanna, our chief designer, pokes her head round the door.

"Fine!" I reply, then burst into tears. She puts an arm round me, and leads me across the hall to her office, where she puts me gently in a chair and makes me a mug of proper tea.

An hour later, I leave her office, feeling consoled and clutching a book.

Twenty-Eight Rules for Getting over a Break-up

Rule One: Don't seek Solace in Drugs or Alcohol

OK.

But *Pêche Deluxe* helps to pass the time. I've got into a bit of a routine, now. Usually after work I wander round Ingelow a bit, then sit in the B and B 'guest room' watching soaps or quizzes on a communal TV until I remember I'm a Philosopher and Lover of Great Art. But when I get up to my room, I don't feel like serious reading, so a drink comes in handy.

It tastes nice, too. Maybe Dr Sharilee-Jayne Goodhart PhD (she's the author of the book) hasn't tried it.

Perhaps I'll send her a bottle.

Rule Two: Sort out The Practical Stuff: your Money, your Home.

Bobby's now being Very Sensible About It All, so this is easy. In return, I don't want a load of money off him. Apparently, that's just as well, as there is little equity in the house. All those borrowings against it, to keep the company growing. Or 'going', anyway. We used to talk about this, so this isn't a surprise.

One day, he calls to say that there's a particular business issue we need to sort out quickly. Forget the legal stuff, it will take forever that way. Some joint shares in Mowatts – he'd like to buy me out.

"That's fine," I reply.

"A quid each?" he suggests.

Dr Sharilee-Jayne Goodhart whispers in my ear (she has bright red lips, I have decided, and wears expensive perfume) that I should get someone to look at this. But my heart isn't in it. I was the one who buggered off, after all. Philosophers take the consequences of their freely chosen actions.

"If you think that's fair…" I say.

Soon after, a cheque arrives for seven thousand pounds. That goes a long way in Ingelow. A deposit on a property, for example.

*

I love 23 Fen Street the moment the agent shows me in.

It's quiet, simple, unassuming. OK, the front door opens straight onto the road. It was advertised as 'two bedroom' but the guest bedroom will only be of use if I have one of the Seven Dwarfs to stay (or one of the Six: I'm not inviting Grumpy, as I can do grumpy on my own). The plumbing makes noises, but that is 23 Fen talking to me in its special language that only it and I can understand, saying, 'Hello, Stella, I'll look after you. I won't criticize you.'

The neighbours seem nice. An old couple on one side; a guy on the other who likes heavy metal but doesn't seem to be around much. (He ran an eye over me when we first met, me leaving the house and him arriving. Then he gave a little shake of his head, which I'm sure was subconscious. Suits me.)

Once I'm properly moved in, I hold a little party to celebrate. People from work, and… Well, just people from work, actually. They bring partners, which hurts a bit, but you can't not ask them. Stuart and Gemma bring a bottle of Champagne, Deanna and Joe a book called *Ten Ways to Brighten up your New Home*. Even IT Richard turns up with someone called Beth; the two of them spend most of the evening on my sofa snogging. It's a fun evening, anyway – as far as I can remember, as I drink too much.

But the bed I finally collapse into is *mine*. The toilet I'm sick into afterwards is *mine*.

Rule Three: Get out there and Meet People

Now I'm sitting in *my* front room, in a chair *I* bought from a charity shop, reading *my* book. 'You may not think so right now,' Dr Sharilee-Jayne Goodhart PhD tells me, 'but you have a lot to offer the world. Everybody has.'

I remind myself that she hasn't actually met me – but she's right: I ought to try.

But don't date yet, Dr Goodhart goes on. Just interact…

She seems to think that people actually enjoy dating and need to be dissuaded from it. For me, she might as well write 'Don't drive rusty six-inch nails, slowly, into your hands.'

Yes, I'm weird.

But Dr G says I must interact. I look around for some group activities.

Bridge.

Line dancing.

Nothing grabs me.

There's a shop I pass on the way to work that sells long velvet dresses, bronze hookah pipes and pictures of sombre-faced Native Americans. One day, I see a poster in the window.

Ingelow Freethinkers invite you to
a talk by Dr Empyrion Pangelides
at the Clement Attlee Hall, South Street
7.30, Tuesday 11th
Entrance £1

I'm nearly late – the Hall is rather hard to find – but there is still room. Quite a lot of room, actually. I take a seat and watch as a few more fellow freethinkers arrive. They all greet each other affectionately. With each hug or handshake I see them share, my desire to belong gets ever stronger. I'm a freethinker, too. I'll fit like a glove!

At about twenty to eight, an elderly man wanders out in front of us, picks up a microphone that starts hooting at him, stands helpless until someone fiddles with some controls, then turns to us. "Good evening, everybody. Welcome to our monthly talk. But first, a few notices…"

There are an awful lot of notices. Several centuries later he announces that the business is concluded, and can we all please welcome tonight's speaker, Dr Empyrion Pangelides.

A muscular, bearded man strides up to the microphone. "Good evening, fellow seekers after truth," he booms. "I am from Outer Space!"

The audience nod politely, and Dr Pangelides looks disappointed.

"I was joking, of course," he continues. "But I might not have been. It's a well-known fact that beings from other worlds have been visiting our planet for many years. Maybe one of them is sitting among us now."

Does he glance at me at this moment, or is that my imagination?

"First slide, please."

A blur appears on the screen behind him, which slowly focuses into an old-master painting of the Annunciation. It is not as beautiful as some of the ones Dr Licht showed us. It is also upside down.

120

When the slide is replaced the right way up, I notice that the Virgin's halo is unusually far above her head.

"This is, of course, a UFO," says Dr Pangelides. "Note the *four* lines of light coming down from the craft," he continues. "Most observers see no significance in this – it's just a piece of artistry; four looks nicer than three or five. But, of course, it is *not* a coincidence. Ancient Masters tell us that there are Four Karmic Forces at work in the universe. The first of these is called Zoanthropism."

Zoanthropism is – well, it's a bit complicated. Something to do with the global psychosystem. All living things have panvibrationary frequencies, which can be endo- or exo-harmonic. Visitors can sense these with ease. Terrestrials can do so if we practice noetic attunement. There's a course Dr Pangelides runs; the next one is in July and there are places still available. There's a special discount for us today.

Then there's astrofluvialism, which only operates at the transformative, or 'Kappa' level. It – Oh, God, my attention begins to lapse at this point. Sorry, Dr Pangelides. Why are these seats so uncomfortable? I think of my nice armchair back home, then how nice it feels to think 'back home'.

"There's been a lot to take in," the Doctor is saying. "Time for a break."

The main lights go on, and a hatch in the right-hand wall flies open. "Tea and biscuits," says a voice from behind it.

Time to socialize!

Who with?

I start sidling along my row. The woman at the end shows no sign of moving, and I come to a halt. Nothing happens. I consider backtracking and going out along the next one, which is empty. Finally, she looks up at me and grins.

"Isn't he interesting?" she says.

"I…"

"There are so many fascinating ideas around nowadays, don't you think? My name's Sarah. With a P."

"Oh, Stella. Stella Tranter."

"Nice to meet you. Let's get some tea." She gives me a knowing look. "We should get in the queue. They sometimes run out of biscuits." We do so. "We are entering a whole new era of love," she says.

"I… guess so."

"Oh, we are, Sheila. The Age of Love is upon us – and not a moment too soon."

I should ask her a question, shouldn't I?

"Do… you come here a lot?" I say finally.

"Oh, yes. We have well-known speakers, you know."

She begins to reel off a list of people I have never heard of, till we get to the front of the queue.

"Sorry," says the woman pouring the tea. "That was the last of the biscuits."

"That's karma," says 'Sarah'.

No, I think, it's because you sat on your fat arse for ages and wouldn't let me past. I nod. "Karma…"

A man with a goatee beard comes up to us.

"Sheila, this is Doug," says Sarah. "He's an expert on geometry."

"Geo – netry," he corrects her.

"Oh, yes, of course. A few months ago, Doug gave a most interesting talk about the pyramids."

"I love the idea of Ancient Egypt…" I begin, but Doug doesn't seem interested.

"The pyramids are magnets for geonetic forces," he says,

122

fixing me with an intense gaze. "I'm hoping this chappie's going to talk about them in the second half. It's been a bit, er, superficial, so far, don't you think?"

"Well, I'm not – "

"The people who built the pyramids possessed technology that was way superior to our own. How do you think huge, forty-ton blocks of stone were raised hundreds of feet above the ground?"

"Perhaps they got lots of slaves to – "

"They used geonetics. The inhabitants of Ancient Egypt, or *Misr* as it should properly be called, used giant gongs, or *hmbs*, made of bronze – the exact formula for their manufacture remains a mystery."

"Maybe – "

"The *hmbs* were struck with giant beaters, or *qlfs*, and the sound waves were directed to drive the stones up ramps of wood, known as *ntpls*. To do this, the waves need to be channeled geonetically. There's no other way."

Doug's mouth seems to move without any other part of his body, even his beard, which looks sillier by the moment, moving. I am overcome with a desire to pull at it, to see if it is real. Fortunately, the old boy who made the announcements then starts pinging the side of a teacup with a spoon and asks us to return to our seats.

"That's *so* fascinating, Doug," says Sarah (with a P? Oh, don't even bother).

"Yes it is," Doug replies.

In the second part of the lecture, we learn the nature of the Third and Fourth Karmic Forces, how these relate to the Twelve Signs of the Zodiac and the Eight Chakras (not seven, as the ill-informed think), then finally the Unifying Principle behind them all, which the Doctor announces is, of course, Love.

"Any questions?" he asks at the end.

Doug's hand shoots up. "I don't quite see how this fits in with the theory – and practice – of geonetics."

"I'm not sure what you mean, sir."

"Surely you know Elliot Q Tandberg's work on geonetry?"

"Geometry?"

"No, Geo-netry. The Science of Geonetics."

"Oh. No. Er…"

"You should read it." Doug then commences a lengthy description of Elliot Q Tandberg's work. After a while, the man who pinged the teacup interrupts. Has anyone else any questions?

Nobody answers.

I see Doug limbering up for another question and feel pity for Dr Pangelides. He may be a total charlatan, but he is still a human being in need of protection from the appalling, all-enveloping self-centredness of Doug. I stick my hand up.

"Why is love so important?" I ask. "It seems to me the most unreliable thing in the world. Is everybody in this room madly in love?"

An embarrassed silence falls.

"The Masters are talking of love on a cosmic scale," says Dr Pangelides.

"What the fuck does that mean?" I snap back.

I didn't mean to, promise. It just came out. Like that kid in *The Omen*…

People either look away, horrified, or turn and stare.

Doug asks another question, and Dr Pangelides suddenly

says he has no more time. Teacup man announces that next month will feature a talk on the Lost World of Atlantis and can we help stack the chairs, please.

I do my bit, but everyone avoids eye contact.

"Shame on you," mutters Nietzsche as I walk home. "How could you even think of attending an event like that? You, a Philosopher?"

Descartes nods in agreement.

I round on them. 'What would you do instead, then? Stuck here in the middle of bloody nowhere because of all this stuff you told me about authenticity and points of certainty? Come on, clever-clogs. Tell me. What… would… you… do? Bridge? Line dancing?'

They fall silent.

"Line dancing might be fun," suggests Descartes.

Nietzsche nods. "Yee-hah!" he adds.

Rule Four. Give Yourself Treats

Dr Sharilee-Jayne Goodhart PhD insists on this.

One day I see a young woman cycling down Southgate Road. She has a joyous smile, but what I like most is the way her hair flies out behind her, a symbol of defiance. Unmanageable? Unfashionable? Who cares? It is hers and it is rebellious and beautiful.

There's a bike shop in the town centre. My Treat – there's a little left over from my shares after the deposit and all the various fees that seem to come with buying one's own place – is sky-blue; she has six gears, a real leather saddle and panniers at the back to put picnics in. She's called a Queen Roadster.

I ride Her Most Regal and Wondrous Majesty around

town, turning a few heads (OK, maybe they're just checking to see if there is any traffic behind me before crossing the road). Better still, I start exploring the flat land that surrounds Ingelow. People say the Fens are ugly and unlovable, but I soon realize they have their own secret beauty. They have huge cloudscapes. They have black fecund earth. They have geometry (no geonetry out here!) Ruler-straight lines of poplars, marching pylons, ditches full of whispering reeds, which lead the eye – and the mind – away to a horizon as distant and mysterious as the sea. Do strange land-spirits live here, ancient and magical?

Rule Five. Remember that you will Slip Back sometimes.

Dr Goodhart talks about 'dips'.

I get a lot of those. Some mornings, I wake up cheerful and stay that way: Alex? Pfah! A walk-on part in my life, whose role was to bring me here so I could start being really true to myself.

But just as often, he barges into my thoughts the moment I wake up. I sense him; I want him. I feel the pain of rejection. That thought, again and again, that it is some kind of mistake.

I know that's wrong, but something in me insists otherwise. I hate myself for this weakness, but…

You just have to ride these dips out, Dr Goodhart says. They are tests of the New You that you are creating.

I get that. The real New Stella, not that infatuated overgrown teenage one. Keen cyclist and lover of the Fens. Conscientious accountant/office manager of Zzapp! Marketing. Responsible property owner at 23 Fen Street.

One day, this New Me is on High Street, heading for the Oxfam shop where she's noticed a rather nice throw to put over her sofa. And who do I see coming out of the town's only record store?

It really is him, too. I've had a number of false sightings, but this is the real thing.

Right, New Stella. Should I:

a) Ignore him

or

b) Saunter up and say 'Hi' in a cheery, I'm-over-*you,*-mate-y sort of way?

Dr G would say that option a) is too passive. Take command!

Yes!

I start sauntering.

A woman follows him out and hands him a bag. He flashes a smile at her and takes her hand. "Poor cow," I chuckle knowingly to myself.

Then someone kicks me in the stomach.

OK, not literally, but that's how it feels. For a moment I want to vomit. I fight that back, turn away and make myself walk, with calm and dignity, back towards Fen Street. The moment I am out of his view, I ditch the calm and dignity and run all the way home, scrabble with the keys, slam the door behind me, sink into my sofa and start sobbing uncontrollably. The sobs are deeper even than those when I first lay on my bed in the B and B. I'm sobbing my soul out.

Why? What the hell's going on?

I'm healing, aren't I? Getting better. Recovering from this brief insanity which is all in the past now. This is a dip.

It isn't a fucking dip it's a precipice and I've just been kicked over it and I don't know why but this is so bloody unfair and it hurts so much and… *Why?*

127

I try to calm myself.

I get slowly to my feet, and they lead me into the hall and place me in front of the mirror that Dr G says I should look into every day and remind myself I am beautiful.

I look in it and see a face made ugly by tears. No, it was ugly before the tears. Horrendously, innately ugly, no-wonder-everyone-rejects-me ugly.

My true self?

Maybe. Or is the truth even worse?

To thine own self be true… Supposing there is nothing to be true to? Maybe the reason that Alex didn't love me was because there wasn't anything to love. Supposing 'I' – the Old I, the New I, the New New I, all the bloody Is that have ever gone round labelled 'Stella Tranter' or 'Stella Mowatt' – supposing these are just an endless succession of selfish, meaningless, momentary needs and emotions? Not Dr Licht's vision, nor Friedrich Nietzsche's, but David Hume's. Me, want, now. That's all. Me, long for, can't have, fall apart. No centre, no purpose, no 'Cartesian' point.

"I don't think I could live if I really thought that," I say.

"No, you probably couldn't," Earl replies.

I let out a yell, which I hope will smash that mirror. It doesn't. I pace round the hall, fists clenched. I hear myself making weird noises. Like demons? No, they are not inside me yet.

But they want to be.

I burst out of the door, unchain the bike with shaking hands, and pedal, pedal, pedal furiously onto South Road and out towards the edge of the town. Demons are after me, the ones that whispered in Descartes' ears that his clever mathematical proofs were illusions, and who are now howling in mine that I am an illusion, too. I storm through a red light, nearly knocking over an old man with two bags of shopping. Sorry, I can't stop. If those demons catch me…

*

I do stop, of course. I stop when I'm exhausted, when I can't pedal another inch, when I'm miles out in the Fens, my beloved Fens; I don't care where, as there's nowhere I'm going anyway.

"All right, take me," I tell the demons as I slump forward over the handlebars, heaving breath in and out of my lungs. "You win. You were always going to, weren't you? That's what happens to non-people like me. Finish me off!" I stretch up, hands to the sky, in a gesture of surrender. In reply…

Nothing happens.

The wind puffs in my face.

A seagull screeches.

I take a long, slow breath and feel it enter my body, then pause. I breathe it out again.

I look around. I'm still here. In this landscape. In my landscape. My skies, my black earth, my geometry, my sea of strangeness.

And what's that on the horizon?

It's the spire of Cawston church.

I expect to feel a second boot to the guts, the *coup de grace* that the demons have been saving up, just for me.

I fill with lightness and joy.

Love. I remember it. Love that *was* real. It wasn't me, me, me, either. My love wanted to give; to inspire, to build, to contribute, to share. And it was so strong! I feel it again, now, pure and full, the first time I've allowed myself to for ages. I love! Here (I rub my abdomen). And here (I clasp my hands to my heart). And here (I rub my fingers across my face and through my hair). And here (I give my whole body a huge, slow caress). It didn't end well, but it was generous and deep and, above all, real.

I loved, therefore I am.

I begin to ride towards the village.

Rule Six, Rule Seven, Rule Eight (and so on).

Pooh, I don't need these. I have a Point of Certainty.

Stalking

I cycle out to Cawston several evenings a week, now. Into the village, across the top of Common Road, then on to North Beach or looping up through the fens to Notby or Sea Pining. I nearly always get a 'moment' like the one where I spotted the spire, when I know I am real after all, not a swirl of meaningless nothingness.

I loved therefore I am…

Yes, of course part of me is aware of how ridiculous this pedalling round in search of Cartesian moments of self-confirmation must seem – to someone else. But *I am a unique being, only once on this earth,* and to me it is the essence of staying whole and real and sane.

I can face myself in the mirror in which I am supposed to be beautiful and at least be true.

When the days shorten, I have to cut my trips down to weekends only. I find I can live with this. Just. During the week I work hard: business is brisk in the world where people make things, sell things, buy things, are Always Positive and dress as Osbert the Oystercatcher. Evenings it's TV or cooking, the recipes complex and engrossing. All in my lovely home. 23 Fen Street, Ingelow. No, there was one moment when it couldn't protect me, but that, I realize, is not its job anyway. I protect myself. In my way.

However, one Sunday I follow my usual bike-route and get no 'moment'.

I tell myself I cannot force them – that's the point; they just come, and that's what makes them meaningful. But what if the supply runs dry for good? Will the nothingness creep up on me and ambush me again one day?

No! I tell myself.

But it might. I don't *know*. (Does anybody know anything? mutters David Hume.)

If it did run out, I'd have nowhere to go.

By Wednesday I can't stand any more, so I take the afternoon off, pleading a migraine, and do the ride. This time I pause at the top of Common Road, take a deep breath and slowly pedal towards Alex's. Opposite number 58, I recall how we once set out on a walk but only got this far when a huge black cloud blew up. I feel that moment of full-on loving and being loved back. I'm fine. I'm real. I have meaning. I loved, therefore I am.

A couple of rides later, this location no longer delivers a moment. The memory has become expected; to really work, it has to surprise me. But that's fine, as I pedal on to number 44 and the garden ornaments – gnomes, windmills, toadstools and wide-eyed cats – that Alex used to be so viciously but wittily rude about, and it is there. A few more visits, and it has to be number 38, with its tatty wooden notice board advertising a British Legion Jumble Sale from eight months ago. Finally, I'm forced to grit my teeth and pedal right past number 26.

But I still know. I loved, therefore I am.

*

One day, his car isn't outside the house.

Curious, I coast to a halt and stare at the front door. Behind it will be the big room: the fireplace, the books, the art, the sofa – where we made love, with all that term means. Turning lust and strangeness into the ultimate affirmation of each other: love.

I find myself wheeling Her Majesty up to the next lamp-post, propping Her up there and walking slowly back.

Crunch, crunch. I'm at the window and can see inside. The rugs. The Persian one he really liked. The red one by the fireplace – for some reason that was my favourite. It's a bit faded, and Alex wanted to throw it out; I said he ought to move it somewhere more central, next to the piano – but didn't, of course.

I spot my reflection in the front of a poster, and jump.

This is getting weird, Stella.

But it is necessary.

I loved, therefore I am.

*

A few weeks later, the car isn't there again. I take Her Majesty over to the lamp-post, lock Her there, walk back… At the side of the house is a weatherboarded gate. There are no sounds from the back garden, so why not take a look? If a car draws up, the sound of the gravel will alert me. There's a hoppable fence at the far end, straight into fields.

The moment I'm through the gate I know this is a brilliant thing to do. Maybe I can gorge myself on memories and not need to come back for a long, long while. That bench we had to be so careful sitting on – he's mended it. For him and someone else to sit on?

Maybe. It doesn't matter. This is about me. *I* loved, therefore *I* am.

The vegetable patch. A bit better ordered now, but still largely full of weeds.

The gnome. Pure post-modern irony, of course; Alex's *hommage* to number 44. He used to keep a back-door key under it.

He still does.

Well, I'm here, aren't I? Why waste an opportunity that may not recur for ages? I know exactly how to fit the slightly rusty but still workable key into the lock, and exactly how far to turn it.

Like this. Click.

I am inside the house.

A quarter-read novel by someone I've never heard of – not that that matters; just my having loved – straddles the arm of his favourite chair. There's cat hair all over the place. The fiddle isn't even in its case, just sitting on top of the piano.

I go over to the sofa and sink into it. I wander into the kitchen, where the same old mugs hang from the same unevenly spaced hooks. *Berliner Musikfest 1987.* He's a bit low on milk, I notice. Oh, God! Maybe he's just popped out to get some more.

No, the village shop is closed on Sundays and he'd hardly go all the way to Ingelow for a pint of milk. When we went out at weekends, it was for long walks. We'd often not get back till it was dark. Sometimes we'd go straight upstairs afterwards…

I climb the stairs and push gently on the bedroom door, sit down on his side of the bed, stroke the pillows, bury my face in them. The smell is instantly familiar.

I loved, therefore I am.

I'm not sure how long I spend up here, then suddenly it is enough. As I turn away, I wonder if this will be a turning point. Maybe I'll never have to come back.

I make my way downstairs again. A last look around. My glance falls on the violin. I want to hold it just one more time. I pick it up, with intense care, and feel its lightness.

The moment I do, I know that all shall be well. I can reconnect with all my noblest aspirations, and move forward. I shall live fully, authentically, by the best standards, the ones I found – or did they find me? – in that funny little room, all those years ago, in The Enlightenment Club. Philosophy and Great Art will support me: me, Stella Tranter, a woman of substance who can love and relish beauty and show others how –

Crunch.

Wheels on gravel.

I jump with fright, and the violin… Well, it just seems to leap out of my hands. I make a despairing grab for it, but that only sets it spinning, so when it hits the flagstones, it does so with extra force. A crack echoes round the room.

Its arched brown back has a long split all the way down the middle.

Stay calm, Stella.

'I just happened to be passing by, and remembered I'd left something behind, and – '

I panic.

Out the back door. Lock. Hide the key. Run!

Walking

I don't stop pedalling till the point where the road rises up and runs over the old sea-wall. There, exhaustion finally gets to me. I stop and dismount – well, virtually fall off – flop onto the grass, then glance back at a very distant Cawston.

Nobody's following.

I sigh with relief, then realize how ridiculous that is. I must go back and explain. A shiver runs through me at the thought of quite how embarrassing that is going to be, but it has to be done. I pick myself up and turn the bike round. I put my foot on the pedal and poise myself to move forward.

Nothing happens.

'Just push down, Stella.'

I can't.

'You're not just going to run away, are you?'

No, I'll...

...*cycle* away. I turn the bike round and coast down the far side of the dike towards the sea.

I tell myself this is cowardly and dreadfully wrong.

I ride on.

At North Beach there's one vehicle in the car park, one of those round-looking ones that old men drive. No sign of its owner. Perfect. As I prop Her Majesty up against a litter-bin, I run a fantasy in my head, that a nuclear war has broken out and destroyed all human life the other side of the sea-wall. Now there's only me and one car-owning old man, and I'll find ways of avoiding him. There will be no more emotional entanglements, nothing more to get wrong, no more embarrassment, no more inadequacy, no more other people to have standards that I fall perpetually short of. A world without people = a world without pain. Simple. Logical.

I walk. The tide is out, but I want to see the sea close-to and be as far from the people-cursed land as possible.

I soon get to the first marks of the October spring tide – just a few days ago, it must have been – plastic bottles, rope, bladderwrack, bleached pieces of wood (one of them looks uncannily like that violin lying broken on the floor). Then I reach a section where shells crunch underfoot. Then these are replaced by beautiful, half-flooded ridges of sand. Then there's a bit where my footings turn to mush. Then it's firm sand again.

I'm now at the start of a spit that juts all the way out into the sea, which is still a long way away, but now audible, a gentle but insistent whoosh. Ahead and to my left, is a kind of lagoon, calm and sparkling. To my right, a miniature cliff drops into a choppy, deep-looking current: the mouth (I guess) of one of the little rivers that wind through the dunes. In front of me, the spit divides, one branch peeling off to the left to enclose the lagoon, while the other forms a peninsula of sand that runs straight out seawards, till it vanishes beneath a criss-cross of breakers.

I follow the latter, setting myself targets – a boulder, which I soon reach; a buoy; a bright-green streamer of kelp. Only at the last of these do I ask myself exactly why I'm doing this, but I get no reply other than that I want to, so walk on.

I am now near the end of my peninsula. Small waves lick either side of me; ahead they merge with deceptive neatness, and beyond that are the real breakers, hurling themselves onto a small ridge of shingle. There's spray in the air now, flying everywhere. The sea makes a range of sounds, as befits what it is now an angry, living thing. There is a boom as a wave topples over, a slow hiss as it unfurls foamy water across the pebbles, a greedy, sensual suck as it retreats to meet the next water-wall rearing up behind it. The wind, which has become strong out here, joins this pandemonium by buffeting my ears.

Soon I am on the shingle-ridge, yards from the line of foam where the waves exhaust themselves. I stand and watch the wind pulling this line apart, sending little parcels of the stuff flying in random directions, till a big roller comes in and buries it. Then one particularly large wave crashes in and drives itself right to the tips of my toes.

I'm filled with a strange, wild happiness, which I do not understand.

Then I do understand.

This is where it must end. The whole bloody charade. The endless loops of running and hiding, the biggest one of which has just reached the perfect negation of its beginning. My dream, of climbing out of mediocrity by finding higher, better things to attune myself to, began in that cramped but glorious little room in the Polytechnic. It has just concluded with my smashing a perfect symbol of everything that room offered.

But it hasn't closed totally. One tiny strand is still loose – and remains mine. I still have choice.

I can choose to crawl, shame-filled, back to land where I will be ripped to shreds, not by mythical demons but by real, even more vicious, human beings for my egotism, weakness and stupidity. Or I can just say fuck it all and merge myself wonderfully with the boundless, roaring power of nature in front of me. One moment of magnificence, and then permanent silence, permanent rest.

I begin to walk into the foam. Ahead, the next breaker is drawing itself up for its self-immolation. Maybe that one will take me; maybe the next. It does not matter.

This is my true Cartesian point.

Boom! The water cascades towards me, and I will it to sweep me away. Merge me with your might! I have chosen to die; gloriously, willed and willing, free – *free!* – at last from –

Don't be such a bloody idiot, Stella!

I've no idea where the voice comes from, but it is loud and clear.

I spin round and begin splashing furiously back towards the land. The wave that has fallen behind me grabs my calves with its ice-cold talons, at first pushing me in my new chosen direction, then, pretence over, dragging me seawards. For an instant, its pull is so strong that I don't think I can resist, but I dig in and then the pressure is gone. When its successor follows, I have outpaced it. Soon I'm on dry, solid beach.

I give a sigh of relief and sink to my haunches, staring out at the sea that is now just a rather noisy thing out there. Beautiful, in its place, but no match for me, as I have will and life and a future. I begin to laugh: great heaving laughs of a kind that I don't think I've ever made before. I have no idea what I am laughing at; then I do know – it is at myself. And if I can laugh at myself then all this nonsense about non-existence is truly ridiculous. I have nothing to prove, just life to live.

Go home, Stella. Sort out the mess you've got yourself into, which is, admittedly, considerable but is sortable because everything is if you put your mind to it. Go and get on with your life, which is true and beautiful and beyond price.

I laugh some more, then rub my eyes. Then I'm ready to

return to confessing to Alex, to explaining and paying for any damage, to finalizing my divorce – which wasn't caused by my rampant egotism but by the simple, sad coming together of two human beings who thought they were made for each other but who turned out not to be. I'll even get 23 Fen Street's plumbing fixed.

I turn and start walking, proud as a cat, towards that crazy, amazing circus we call life.

Oh.

While I was busy having my existential revelations, the tide sneaked in between me and the land, covering the 'peninsula'. There must be twenty yards of water, now, with no clue as to the lie of the sand beneath it. I know that to the left, the ground tumbles into what will now be a current-filled channel. I recall that to my right the footings were soft and treacherous. So I just have to head straight, I suppose. But will it be that simple?

When the tide comes in, it's so fast.

Just do it, Stella. And quickly, or it will be too late.

I start wading, and soon head too far right and find myself in gloop. So left a bit, but not too far – fall into that channel and I am gone: dragged down, choking, struggling – a clumsy, unwilling version of the fate I longed for a few minutes ago but now view with horror. I wonder if I'll see my life flash before me, and if so, how I will feel about it all.

No!

More steps. All good so far. But then I feel the pressure around my feet getting stronger.

Ignore it. Keep walking.

I am, I guess, about half-way across when a wave smacks into my calves and nearly knocks me over. I turn and see breakers rolling across open water where that nice enclosed lagoon once was.

So? I just have to keep going. I have no choice. The thought comes, that maybe freedom is not about having choice but about *not* having choice. It is knowing that you have to fight for something with every atom of your body, and then simply just doing that. I won't go down without a fight – now, or ever again.

I brace myself for the next wave, take its pressure, then have a few moments to shuffle forward before the next one hits. I curse it, and my fury gives me energy.

Keep going, Stella. Step, brace, take the next wave.

Step – it's deeper– am I going too far left? I try and look through the rushing water but it's hopelessly unclear. So I must fix my eyes on a landmark – that old car is perfect. Head for it, and hope. Brace. Take the pressure…

The water swirls round me. It roars. Its spray stings my eyes, and is making my clothes damper and colder with every moment. Brace, take the pressure, step – Please God, let there be enough time (please *who*, Stella? Shut up and get on with it). No deeper, thankfully. Brace, take the pressure, step –

Help! I tumble forward; my hands scrabble for sand and find it. Water cascades over me. I feel it lift my body and heave me forward, but mercifully not into the channel. I hack out a lungful of brine and force myself back to my feet, just in time to withstand the next onslaught. But I'm shaking now. I'm sodden. Shivering. I start to wonder which wave will get me. This one? The one after that? The one after that? Dry land seems further away than ever – it *is* further away than ever, because the tide is pouring in, driven by the mighty moon and the huge weight of the North Sea. The water between that land and me is deepening every second.

Keep moving!

Brace, take the pressure, step. My body is screaming that it can't go much further. I scream back at it that it bloody well can and bloody well will, and that seems to stop its complaining – for another step at least. And another. But I can't scream myself safe for ever. Brace, take the pressure…

The next minutes feel like a lifetime.

Brace, take the pressure, step.

Maybe they are a lifetime.

Brace, take the pressure, step.

Then, suddenly, my next step is clearly shallower.

Don't get your hopes up. Keep fighting.

The next one is shallower still.

You've not there yet, Stella. Keep at it.

Another big wave comes in. Brace, take the pressure. I roar insults at it, and it is past me. I step forward again, confident suddenly.

And then it is over. The waves are spending their intensity behind me and I'm striding through the water, splashing in shallows, yelping and whooping with the joy of a child.

Someone has appeared on the beach. I fall silent, suddenly embarrassed. The person runs towards me. He stops by the water's edge and holds out a hand; I stagger up to him and grasp it.

"Are you all right?" he says.

"Fine, thanks." Of course I'm fine.

Who does he think I am? Some idiot who lets herself get caught by the tide?

I collapse at his feet.

Falling

I'm sitting in the old car, wrapped in a travelling-blanket; the engine is running and the heater on full blast; I've got water all over *Seabirds of Britain*, drunk all this man's coffee and eaten both the jam doughnuts he'd bought for his tea.

"I still think I'd better take you to the hospital," he says.

"No. I just need to get home, that's all."

"You're sure?"

"Yes. I'm already amazingly grateful for what you've done."

"We all have to do our bit, don't we?"

"I… guess we do."

We set off.

"What happened to you?" he asks, just as the car is coming up to the old sea wall.

"I didn't notice the tide coming in behind me. I'm new round here."

We reach the top of the wall, run along it for a few yards, then begin our descent.

"Actually, that's rubbish," I go on. "I tried to kill myself. Then I suddenly realized what a bloody stupid idea that was."

He nods. "Very wise. I got very depressed when my wife died a few years ago. I'm not sure it got as bad as walking out into the sea – but I felt pretty low. I went and saw a therapist. She got me to face up to things. Well, to face up to myself really… She gave me some business cards. I don't think I've got one on me, but I can drop one round to you if it would help."

"That would be kind," I say, though I have this deep

sense I won't need therapy. Not now I've faced the moon and the North Sea. But I give him my address anyway.

"It's always worth battling on, you know," he adds.

"Yes, I do know."

*

The moment I get home, I make a cup of tea, have a hot shower in an element that surely can't be the same as the sea, then flop joyfully onto my bed. I am asleep almost at once. I do not dream, but wake in the middle of the night.

I look round at the window and the ghostly outlines of my little bedroom.

I am experiencing these things.

I am alive. I'm breathing, I'm sentient, I'm dry, I'm warm, I'm here, I'm Stella.

I am, therefore I am.

*

Alex.

It has to be done.

Her Majesty is still out at the beach, so I take the bus to Cawston. I think of the woman who used to cycle along this route, desperate for a moment of sanity amid the madness that swirled around her, and feel pity for, and complete distance from, her.

But of course I still feel nervous as hell.

The bus stops outside the Crusoe Arms. Nobody else gets off. As I walk down Common Road, I try to do so with confidence and calm. He'll understand, I tell myself. It was an accident. Maybe he'll appreciate my honesty in coming forward. I want him to know what I've been through in the last few months. Not to make him guilty, but simply to tell the truth. My truth, shared and worth hearing.

Then the nerves stab back in. He'll hate me. Do I have to do this?

To give myself one last piece of determination, I imagine wading through that water. *I won't go down without a fight – now, or ever again.* I crunch across the gravel and knock on the door.

It opens. Alex is looking at me with a puzzled expression. "Hello…"

"Hello, Alex. I've come to apologise."

He says nothing for a moment, then his jaw drops.

"It was you… Jesus Christ!"

"I'm so terribly sorry, Alex."

"Sorry…?"

"Yes, I… It's awful, I… didn't mean…" I'm getting incoherent.

"You bitch," he says, slowly and clearly. "You fucking bitch. I… can't think of anything more horrible than that, Stella. Anything more egocentric, more petty, more vindictive, more spiteful, more – " He begins to lose it, then calms himself.

"It was an accident, Alex," I say, calming myself, too.

"An accident? What do you mean?"

"It wasn't deliberate. You don't think I…? You can't…"

"What were you doing in my house?"

"Yes, I know it sounds odd. I just happened to be passing by, and remembered I'd left something behind, and as you weren't exactly friendly when we parted company, I thought if I let myself in and took it, that way there'd be less embarrassment and…"

I stop.

"No," I say. "The truth. I was going crazy. There was this hideous emptiness inside, and the only way I could stop it eating me up was to – "

"Oh, for God's sake," he says, and slams the door. His voice calls out from behind it: "Wait there, please."

I rehearse the story. He has to know. Maybe start at the record shop, or how I felt when I saw the spire, or…

He's back at the doorway, holding out a piece of paper at arm's length. "Read this and sign, please."

I take it; the moment it is in my hand, he pulls his away with a gesture of revulsion.

I, Mrs Stella Mowatt, née Tranter, am responsible for the damage for the Donati violin and will pay for any repairs necessary or for a replacement if the instrument is irreparable.

"Well, of course I'll do that, Alex. That's part of what I've come round to say. I don't need to sign a piece of – "

"Sign it."

"I haven't got a pen."

"Don't get clever with me. Wait there. If you're not there when I get back, I'm calling the police."

"Alex…" I protest, but the door has already shut.

I stare at it till it opens again. "Here." Alex is shoving a pen in my direction.

"Thank you," I say, out of habit, then sign the paper. "Look. It all started when – "

"I'm not interested, Stella."

"I want you to understand!"

"I want you to fuck off out of my life and never have anything to do with me again. Anything. Ever. Now give me that bit of paper back."

I hold on to it for a moment, realizing that it gives me power. Then I hold it out and he snatches it. Power to do what?

146

"This was you to a tee, wasn't it, Stella?" he says. "The real you. Deep down inside, you loathe culture for being beyond you. You're worse than those dickheads in Ingelow who ignore it altogether – at least they stick to their melodramatic soap operas and whining Abba records, and don't pretend that they belong anywhere else." He grimaces. "But you… You, Stella, are the ultimate phoney, the ultimate enemy of all that is good and truthful. Your narcissistic, empty little ego lies its way into somewhere it thinks is shiny and beautiful, then systematically sets about dragging everything around it down to its own infinitely vacuous and selfish level. You should have stayed with your pompous, adolescent punk rock band or your dull, golf-playing little husband, instead of trying to fool everyone with your ridiculous Philosophy and Great Art act."

He smiles, though not at me. This smile is for internal consumption only.

"I guess I'm grateful to you in some way, for showing me how deep some people can sink. It's quite a consolation really. But don't think this means I'm going to just walk away. You will get that fiddle fixed. You will put back every little bit of decency and truth you have tried to suck out of the world."

The smile broadens. "You'll probably hate doing so. I hope you do, Stella. God, I hope so. I hope you wake up every morning feeling acutely aware of how small you are and how big the world of True Art and True Beauty is and how you will never get close to it in a hundred years, however hard you try, because you just don't have it in you. And I hope it hurts like hell. Every damned moment of it." He pauses. "My solicitor will be in touch. Now fuck off."

The door slams.

"You're wrong," I say to it. But my voice has no strength.

So I simply stand and stare at the door, then turn and trudge back to the bus stop. There's another one in three hours.

*

I must say sorry properly. Show him that those things he said aren't true. I sit at my desk and fill my waste-paper basket with versions.

I manage something decent, finally. Something human, real and not self-pitying, but not bland or pushy either. Something really 'me'. I walk to the end of Fen Street and balance the letter on the lip of the postbox, recalling how I felt when I first wrote to

26 Common Road

Cawston

Ingelow

AT29 8QX

"Bring calm and peace," I ask it. "For both of us."

*

The reply comes a week later.

P. Sproule represents Alex Collings of 26 Common Road, Cawston, Ingelow, AT29 8QX. She has a document, signed by me, admitting damage to her client's property and accepting all liability. Repairs have not proven possible. Sourcing and purchasing a replacement instrument of commensurate quality will cost £20,000. Will I please contact the office to arrange payment. In the case of non-compliance, a criminal complaint will be made to the police and formal proceedings to obtain the monies will be commenced forthwith and pursued with full force of the law (and so on for several pages).

On Saturday I go down to London and visit some music shops. £20,000 for a Donati is 'a bit on the high side', I learn, but it's hard to price quality instruments. One man who seems interested in my story tells me that I need to check that the violin is totally irreparable: restorers can do great work these days. He also recommends I get legal help.

First thing Monday morning, I get out the Yellow Pages.

"Can you hold a moment please?" says the receptionist from the first solicitors I call.

Music begins. Vivaldi's *Four Seasons*. Violin music.

I put the receiver down.

Come on, Stella! *I won't go down without a fight – now, or ever again.* Remember?

But fighting would prove him right. It was my fault, after all, even if it wasn't the deliberate act of vandalism he has decided it was. It was my doing, so I'll pay the price.

Hell, it's only money.

*

"It's only money!" I say jokily.

My bank manager gives me a look as if I'd just announced I was from another planet and did he mind if I parked my UFO in his ashtray. "It's a great deal of money, Mrs Mowatt."

"Yes, but… I have to have it. I've said why."

He glances at the sheet I've filled in, showing my assets, liabilities, income and outgoings. "We can't lend against your property, I'm afraid, as you do not have sufficient equity. Is there any other asset of substance you have not mentioned on this list?"

"I've got a nice bicycle," I say sarcastically.

"Family funds?"

"My mother rents. My sister… doesn't really 'do' money. Anyway, it's up to me."

The manager nods. "If you were to release the equity in your property by selling it, and use that to pay a proportion of your debt, that would bring your liability down to a level where we could consider an unsecured loan. At a suitable rate, of course. You must understand that loans without – "

"You mean I have to sell my house?" I cut in. "My lovely house?"

"Yes," he says. Just that.

"And where will I live?"

"There is a reasonably liquid rental market in the town, Mrs Mowatt."

I tell him I'll think about it, then wander idly through town hoping a magical escape route will present itself. But of course there are no such routes, just estate agents.

TO LET: Mobile Home.

It doesn't look too awful.

*

I make sure I'm out when the agent shows prospective buyers round 23 Fen Street. How could I face them, these thieves trying to take the one thing left to me?

These people who will get me out of the hole that I dug myself into, I remind myself. But I still can't face them.

An offer is made.

"It's a bit on the low side, but it's a buyer's market at the moment," the agent tells me.

After the survey, the prospective purchaser tries to beat me down further because of the state of the plumbing. On the same day, I get a letter from Alex's solicitors chasing a first instalment I promised. Mr Collings will refer the matter to the police if the monies are not paid.

"He's awfully determined," the lawyer admits in a rare moment of candour, when I call her to explain my situation. "Were you really horrible to him?"

*

I spend my first evening in 57 Sunny View Park, noticing how damp the place is and listening to the couple next door having a row.

I don't care. I got myself into this mess; I'll get myself out of it.

And at least I still have my work.

*

A week or so later, Stuart bounds into the office saying that we are sponsoring a group of musicians called the Fenland Orchestra and isn't this a wonderful opportunity to raise the profile of the business. I can't remember my exact comment, but he replies that I'm being negative. Zzapp! Marketing is a Negativity-Free Zone, he reminds me. I apologise.

Two days later, Stuart says that the orchestra has decided to go with another sponsor, Fizz Publicity. Apparently one of their committee went crazy when he heard about the deal, and insisted on changing.

"I don't know what we did wrong," he says, with a shrug.

Just before Christmas, he calls me into the office again. One of our biggest clients is moving their account to Fizz. The MD is a great fan of classical music and has been particularly impressed by what Fizz are doing with the orchestra. As a result, Zzapp! are having to cut back. He's so sorry. I've been a great team member. They'll pay me till the end of the month.

151

They give me the rest of the day off, too. I ride out to North Beach. Well, I creak, as my new bike isn't a patch on a Queen Roadster: Her Majesty had disappeared when I went back to fetch Her. I come here quite a lot. It has become a place of solace, a place of self-renewal, a place where, when things get tough, I can remind myself of how much worse they could have been.

I sit on the sand, stare out at the sea – and feel no solace or self-renewal at all.

"Hello again."

I turn round. It's my bird-watcher.

"Did you go and see Louisa?" he asks.

"No, er, I lost the card. I, er…"

"It took me a while to pluck up the courage, too."

"It's not…" I begin.

"I'll drop another one round. Somewhere on Fen Street, weren't you?"

"I've moved. 57 Sunny View Park."

"Oh. I'm sorry to hear that."

"They're really quite nice, those mobile homes."

He doesn't look convinced.

Roaring

The bike makes a snickering sound as I wheel it up the path, as if it's delighted at quite how hard it has made my journey here. By the doorbell is a little brass plaque telling me I've come to the right place.

Louisa Reid, Therapist.

I park next to a large black wheelie bin and secretly hope that the dustmen will come in the next hour. Then I return to the doorbell, where I pause for a moment. Do I really want this?

I close my eyes and press. There is a deep ring from inside the house. Footsteps.

"Stella?"

Louisa Reid, Therapist, is wearing a floaty skirt, which I totally expected. She is old. Too old? But she has a kind face. Too kind? I wonder if she will be able to take what I have become. Perplexed teenagers, yes. Old women who have lost their husbands, yes. But stalkers who go round smashing vintage musical instruments…

"Do come in," she says gently. "Can I take your coat?"

I hand it over, nervously. Does she have a secret line to men in white coats, for when the really weird ones show up?

"This way!" she says cheerfully, and shows me into an airy room where she invites me to choose a seat from a circle of three. We run through a few procedural matters – payment, confidentiality – then she smiles, adjusts her posture and looks me in the eye.

"So, Stella, tell me about yourself."

"Well…" I begin, then dry up. The room is not airy at all, but crammed full of embarrassment.

"In your own time," Louisa says.

The embarrassment is forcing itself down my throat. I feel myself reddening. I start to sweat again.

"It's nothing," I say suddenly, adding a forced laugh. "I'm fine. I don't know why I came here, really. Just curious, I guess. Nice room you've got here. Those curtains…"

Louisa fixes me with a stare. "Tell me about yourself, Stella," she says firmly.

"I… It's… I'm…"

I burst into tears.

Once I've dried my eyes and begun talking, I can't stop. Alex, seeing him coming out of that shop, the stalking, that bloody violin ("You're going to tell me I smashed it on purpose subconsciously, aren't you?" I say, and Louise shakes her head), Bobby, the Poly, nihilism, Dr Licht, Philosophy and Great Art, and –

"Our time's nearly up, Stella."

"What? An hour?"

"Fifty-five minutes. I have another client coming at six."

"Bloody hell. I've just talked, haven't I?"

"Yes. Talking is good."

"It is, isn't it?" I smile, then look at her earnestly. "So what's wrong with me?"

"You are depressed, I think."

"So I need to cheer up?"

"You need to change, Stella."

"What to?"

"I've no idea. My job is to help you find out."

*

154

"I want you to roar, Stella."

It's our second session, about half way through. Louisa tells me to stand up, stretch out my hands into space and make the loudest noise I can.

I do my best.

She looks dismissive. "That's not roaring, Stella. That's saying the word 'roar'. I mean really roar. With joy. From your very depths."

"Supposing I don't feel any joy or have any depths?"

"Pretend you do."

"All right." The sooner it's finished, the sooner I can get back to telling him about getting ditched by Malcolm.

I roar.

"How did that feel?" Louisa asks.

Actually it was rather nice, but I don't want to let her win that easily. "Yeah. OK."

"Then you won't mind doing it again. Even louder this time."

All-bloody-right. "Roar! Roar! Roar bloody roar, bloody RRROOOAAARRR! Happy with that?"

"You seemed to be, which is what matters. I recommend doing that every day."

"The neighbours would hear."

"Let them. Now, this Malcolm fellow…"

I don't care any longer. It was a long time ago.

At the end of each session, she gives me homework to do. Along with my daily roar, I have to give myself a weekly treat, like going to the cinema or taking a walk in surroundings I find beautiful. I have to keep a diary of 'affirmative' thoughts that leap into my mind, and write them on post-it notes then stick them around my home or at work. She suggests some:

I am a decent person.

Nice people can make mistakes.

Life is a never-ending stream of change.

"These are so Californian!" I protest.

"I know," she replies. "People have all this fun in California, don't they? Sitting on beaches, playing guitars, enjoying the sunshine. Ugh! We're so much classier here in Britain, aren't we? We can be really miserable. That shows how deep we are, doesn't it? So Artistic, so Philosophical."

"Fuck off." (Louisa says I shouldn't hold back in expressing myself.)

But during the week that follows, the caravan fills up with notes.

I quite like them, actually. No, Nietzsche probably didn't have *'I'm OK and other people are OK too'* (in German, of course) stuck on his bathroom door. But would he have been happier if he had done? Maybe he would even have made it with Lou? Or at least grown a more sensible moustache…

I get in my daily roars, too. Not as loud as Louisa would like, but she lives in a solid brick house, not one whose walls seem to have been made of plastic.

*

We don't just talk and roar; we do what Louisa calls 'interventions'. One time I have to hit some pillows to 'get in contact with my anger'.

I give them a gentle tap.

"I don't want to damage them," I explain, when she says I should hit them harder.

"Pretend you do."

"I'm not here to pretend," I snap back, and whack the things, out of frustration, not because this woman has told me to do so. But it does feel rather good, so I do it again. And again. And again…

"I needed some new ones anyway," she says at the end.

"Sorry about the language," I reply.

She grins. "I enjoyed it. You have quite a vocabulary."

Other times she has me sitting on a third chair pretending to be a string of 'significant others' in my life: Lucy, Mother, dad (who has little to say), Anna, the Doctor, the guitarist in Lucy's band, Malcolm, Bobby, Alex (who still takes more time than anyone), Mozart, Descartes, Nietzsche, Lou Andreas-Salome, David Hume, Élisabeth-Louise Vigée Le Brun, God (Louisa says it's best to cast the net wide).

These interactions can get pretty weird. I stick Descartes in a factory farm because of what he thought of animals. I grab the feather from Élisabeth-Louise's hat and start tickling David Hume with it. Sometimes I take two roles. God and Nietzsche have a real ding-dong, one calling the other a Nazi and the other covering his ears and shouting 'You don't exist anyway so I'm not listening to you'.

OK, I'm the one that's weird. But I care less and less. Outside the therapy room, I find happiness seeping into my life. It comes in unexpected places, uninvited.

At work, for example. I've got a temp job in a food-processing factory, not plucking endless chickens, thank God, but doing accounts, which sometimes makes me feel like one of those people who kept records at concentration camps, but which at other times keeps me interested. I do like numbers. They don't hurt anyone.

Or walking, which I do a lot of. Round the town, along the river. Sometimes people say 'Hello' to me, and I always respond. That feels nice. Human. OK, it's not the deepest connection we are capable of, but it's safe. The deep connections are the ones that hurt.

Happiness often takes the form of suddenly realizing I've not been miserable for a while. Then the pain kicks in. Saturday evenings can be bad. I suddenly feel the old fear of nothingness prowling round the caravan, trying to get in. But then it disappears, as suddenly and irrationally as it came. I even go to the door, throw it open and take a series of deep breaths, relishing the fact that there's nothing 'out there' but good, life-giving air.

Life is a never-ending stream of change.

To what?

Louisa claims he has no idea – it's my journey, she says – but I don't believe her. What does she know that I don't?

*

One session, I ask her what the philosophy is behind what she is doing.

"These sessions are about you, not me," she replies.

"That's therapy-speak."

"I'm a therapist."

"I need an answer."

"Why?"

"I just do."

"I'm interested in why you need to know this, Stella."

"Oh, for God's sake, Louisa, I just want to know, OK? Will you please tell me?"

"All right. Do the roaring exercise again."

I do, at full volume plus a bit so she can't complain that I'm not trying properly.

"That's my philosophy," she says when I'm done.

*

At the end of that session, I have to go into her study to write her a cheque for the next six ones.

The room only has one bookshelf, on which sit a number of rather dry-looking texts on therapy, a set of thrillers, some cookery books and a Manual of Home Improvement. No great literature or philosophy.

In the corner is a CD holder, a tall wire rectangle with a wire cat's head on the top and wire cat's paws sticking out of the side – a gift, I assume, from a grateful but taste-deficient client. I check out the contents.

Louisa has them in alphabetical order. So the Abba CDs are at the top. Above Phil Collins, Christopher Cross, Neil Diamond…

I glance up at the mantelpiece, where a familiar sight greets me: a red-roofed cottage, a wagon crossing a stream.

I tell myself that when my bike needs repairing, I don't ask if the repairer reads classic literature, listens to Mozart or has original taste in art.

*

"You don't listen to classical music, do you, Louisa?"

It's about five minutes into the next session.

"No."

"Why not?"

"These sessions are about you, not me, Stella."

"Louisa…"

"OK. I find it rather dull."

"Dull?"

"Yes, dull. You've taken a peek at my CD collection, I assume, so you know what I enjoy. 'Soft adult contemporary' is the official industry classification, I believe. I find the music reassuring after dealing with people's pain all day. Did you like the holder? I got it in a second-hand shop."

"It's… different."

She nods. "I'm afraid classical music doesn't reassure me enough I find it repetitive and rather… tinkly."

"Tinkly?"

"Yes, tinkly. Sorry, I can't think of a better word. Of course, Alex wouldn't approve of those sentiments, would he?"

"No."

"Or Dr Stanislas Licht."

"No."

"Or Wolfgang Amadeus Mozart."

"Well, obviously not."

"And Stella?"

I pause. "No," I say finally but firmly.

"Good. It's one of the things I like most about my work: no two human beings are the same. So why should we all like the same books, or paintings, or music?"

"Great Art is… superior," I say.

"That's an opinion."

"It's a truth," I reply.

"Who says?"

An answer forms, then seems to die on my lips.

"Some philosopher?" she suggests.

"No," I snap, then add, "Well, yes. But what's wrong with that answer?"

"My experience is that whenever someone starts talking about philosophy, they're trying to hide something. It's called over-intellectualization."

"So Descartes and Nietzsche were just 'trying to hide something'?" I say witheringly.

"I don't know. I've never had them sitting in this room. But I'm not very impressed by what you've told me. This business about having one point of certainty in one's life? Why, for heaven's sake?"

"Because, logically, there is no alternative."

"Maybe logic is wrong, then." Louisa gives a shrug. "Supposing there are hundreds of points of certainty? Or none at all, just life, going on all round you, which you're best off just living?"

"So don't ask questions; just be dim-witted and accept everything everybody says?"

"Ask loads of questions, be highly intelligent, don't accept anything if you don't want to – but don't expect a pat, logical answer to emerge at the end. Just live!"

"How?"

She shrugs again. "Do things you like doing. Be nice to people. Smile: did you know that people who smile a lot live an average of 5.3 years longer than those who don't?"

"Gosh, how deep," I say, even more witheringly .

"OK, that was a little homely. But it's better than 'Be utterly selfish. To thine own ego be true'."

"That's not what the Doctor meant! He meant…"

It suddenly occurs to me that I don't know what he meant any longer. Does that matter?

"I sense you're afraid that if there wasn't this great logical structure in place, everything would fall apart," Louisa says. "But maybe it wouldn't. Maybe there's enough vitality and goodness in the world – and in you, Stella – to hold it all together."

"Supposing there isn't?"

"Supposing you just have to trust?"

"Trust what?"

"Just trust."

"That's nihilism!"

"No, Stella. Nihilism is *not* trusting."

I pause to take this in. "You think philosophy is a waste of time, don't you?"

Louisa shakes her head. "Only if it stops you living life well and richly. I'm sure it can be… very interesting. My older brother Felix derives enormous pleasure from his collection of stamps. He's got hundreds of them, all neatly arranged in countries and categories and 'mint' and used and – "

"Philosophy opened wonderful doors for me," I snap.

"You're using the past tense, Stella."

Looking

I have to do this.

I take a couple of days off work. On the first afternoon, I visit Mother: she tells me how she saw Bobby on Dulwich Common the other day. He's doing very well, now. Ever since that firm of his was taken over by Americans. Didn't I have some shares? He's seeing Bill Carr's younger sister, now, by the way. Such a nice, sensible girl. Down to earth...

"That's great news," I interrupt. "Do congratulate him... No, maybe best not. But I'm really happy – for both of them."

Mother shakes her head. "I don't understand you, Stella. I really don't."

That makes two of us. But I don't need more negativity: tomorrow, I must be clear-headed and bright-spirited. I head off to the cheap B and B I've found near the old Crystal Palace, then next morning walk to my destination.

*

KNOWLEDGE FOR ALL.

The old inscription is still above the gate, though harder to read than it was in 1974. Above it is a neon sign welcoming me to the U IVERSIT O CATF RD.

I feel a lump in my throat. Of excitement? Of loss? Or maybe I'm just irritated by the fact that they can't be bothered to fix their bloody sign.

Reception is empty, so I pause to remind myself of the way to the Music Department, then go there. The corridor is a tasteful beige and has been newly carpeted. From the Departmental Secretary's office comes a soft whirring. I knock at the door. No reply. I pause, recalling the last time I stood here, then knock again louder. Still no answer. I push the door and it opens to reveal a girl who looks about 12 encased in a set of earphones. She looks up at me, removes the phones, smiles and asks if she can help.

"I'm trying to find Dr Stanislas Licht," I say proudly.

"Licht?"

"Yes. This is the Music Department, isn't it?"

"Music?" She looks at me as if I have asked for Splidgology or Advanced Pogglorifics. "This is Business Studies. I don't think we have a Music Department…"

"Music…" she says again, still baffled. Then her eyes light up. "One of our lecturers wrote something about conflict over identity in the record industry. *Is the artist always the brand?* it was called. Rather interesting. Is that what you're after?"

"No… I'm sorry… Thanks anyway."

I walk slowly back down the corridor – past the Doctor's old office. The door is half-open and there's nobody inside. I can't resist.

It looks about twice the size I remember it, but I guess that's because all those books have gone – as have the piano, the violin, the music stands, the scores, the loose sheets of music paper, the reels of tape, the bust of Wolfgang Amadeus Mozart and the tape-recorder with Bakelite buttons. Now it is sparse, tidy and smells of air freshener. OK, there are some books: they are on finance and have been corralled onto two shelves which they share with a coffee machine and a photo of a rather drunk-looking group of men.

I sit down on a plastic chair and close my eyes. I can hear the Doctor's voice now:

In their heart, everyone knows well enough that they are a unique being, only once on this earth, and by no extraordinary chance will such a marvellously picturesque piece of diversity in unity as this ever be put together a second time. That's you, Anna, and you, Stella…

I feel the thrill again. I move the chair to where I used to sit. Next to me would be Anna. My fellow-traveller from my first lecture. Where is she now?

Not divorced, unloved, temping, in debt, living in a caravan and seeing a therapist for depression, I suspect.

Another voice:

Deep down inside, you loathe culture for being beyond you. You're worse than those dickheads in Ingelow who ignore it altogether – at least they stick to their melodramatic soap operas and whining Abba records, and don't pretend that they belong anywhere else…

I start scrabbling in my bag for a handkerchief.

"Are you OK?" A young man in a Lacoste T-shirt and white trousers has entered the room.

"Yes – I'm sorry – I – It's…"

"Let me get you a drink of water."

Suddenly I have to tell him all about Dr Licht and the group.

He listens with increasing fascination. "Gosh, I wish I had that effect on my students," he says finally. "We still have a philosophy department here. Would you like to visit them?"

"No."

"You should. I'll take you over there. My name's Julian, by the way."

"Oh… Stella."

We head down the corridor.

"Look, I really don't want to go to the philosophy department," I say as we reach the first set of swing doors. "They… didn't approve of the stuff I just told you about. They caused trouble, and got the course cancelled, actually."

"Even more interesting. What was this guy's name again?"

"Licht."

"We must try and find him."

"We?"

We try the phone book and directory enquiries – no joy – and end up in the office of the University HR Department, looking through old employment records.

"Here we are. Licht, Dr Stanislas. 38 Somersham Road."

Of course!

"And there's a phone number – even though it's an old 01 one…"

We call its updated version, but it is unobtainable.

"I'll go round there," I say.

"I can take you there, if you like."

"No. I…" Julian has become entranced by the Licht magic, but I must go alone, just me and my confusion and pain. He looks disappointed when I tell him this. I try to explain, probably fail, and offer to buy him lunch afterwards instead, promising to report back what I have found.

*

It's a bus ride (still the 197) then a short walk to Somersham Road – just as it was all those years ago when Anna, Noddy and I went to see him. The street is drab, though a few houses have clearly been smartened up. One has a big yellow skip outside it full of rubble, old carpet and bits of furniture.

Number 38 is one of the drab ones. I knock on the dusty, peeling door, which might have once been blue but is now a street-grime grey.

No answer. I try and peep through the windows, but they

are filthy. I knock a few more times. Silence.

I try the neighbours either side. Nobody in. Then a house across the road. Finally, another knock on grubby old 38. No reply.

This is pointless.

∗

Julian insists we lunch in the Senior Common Room. "There might be some old-timers who remember your Doctor." We join a queue. "Any faces you remember?"

I look around. "No."

"What about names? Who taught you?"

"Well, there was Dr Peabody."

"Never heard of him."

I feel a vengeful delight: I may have turned out a loser, but *your* reputation hasn't lasted either, has it, Peabrain?

I try and think of some more names. "Dr Spiggott?" I say, though he's probably teaching in North Korea these days.

"Of course!" says Julian. "I should have thought of him. David Spiggott-Jones has been here for ages. Head of the Economics Department. One of the most radical free-market thinkers in the country."

"Different guy," I laugh.

"No, same guy. He underwent a conversion in the eighties. *The Marxian Myth Exposed. The Great Leap Backwards: the Crimes of Chairman Mao.* You could ask him about Dr Licht if you like. He's over there."

"You mean the one with the quiff and the bow tie?"

"That's him."

"I can't believe it!"

"It's true."

Looking at him now, it is true. Rewild his hair, stick on a

beard and a droopy moustache, find some old jeans… The moment we get our food and find a table, I'm across to where the former Dr Dave Spiggott is tapping at one of these new PowerBook laptops.

"Oh, er, excuse me… Professor Spiggott-Jones… You don't know me, but I'm hoping you can help me."

He glances up and eyes me with a look of distaste.

"I'm… trying to trace an old lecturer here," I continue. "Dr Stanislas Licht. You were a young member of staff when he retired. Do you remember him?"

"No." The professor returns to his PowerBook.

I turn round. Julian is flapping his hands at me in a gesture that I assume means something like 'don't be such a total and utter coward!'

"I'm such an admirer of your work, Professor. *The Marxian Myth Exposed* really spoke to me."

"Which part in particular?"

"Oh, all of me… I was *so* hoping you might remember something about Dr Licht."

"What did he teach?"

"Music."

"We got rid of that lot ages ago."

"This *was* ages ago. There was a particular incident where he got into trouble for running an extra-curricular philosophy course."

"I don't remember, I'm afraid." He goes back to his computer.

"That's such a disappointment. I so enjoyed *The Great Leap Backwards*."

He lets out a sigh and stares into space. "I do recall something. The extra-curricular stuff. Irrationalism.

Dangerous. The powers that be stopped him, of course… And some silly little girl kicked up a huge fuss about it. We had to throw her out. Just as well; she was a militant Trotskyite who'd have had us all hanging from lamp-posts."

"Do you know what happened to him?"

"Sorry. I really have no idea. He's probably sitting in a home for retired liberal arts lecturers in Eastbourne doing the *Guardian* crossword. Subsidized by you and me, in our capacity as taxpayers, of course. I'm assuming you pay tax; you don't look like a sponger."

"Can you think of any way I might find him?"

"I really can't. I'm sorry." He goes back to the computer.

"Well, it was worth a try," says Julian. "Do you want some pudding? The treacle tart is actually quite reasonable."

He gives me a spare key to his room – he's lecturing this afternoon, then has a meeting with a software consultancy interested in sponsoring part of a new MBA – and tells me to 'make myself at home'. I sit there with a mug of coffee from Julian's machine (he reckons the stuff from the SCR is even worse than what you get in the student refectory).

I remember listening to the Requiem as a young man, and suddenly knowing that I had found something that I could build my life around. Something solid, something absolute, a glowing source of inner power that would never let me down.

Then I'm sitting on my sofa in 23 Fen Street, feeling that hideous nothingness. I see the smashed violin on Alex's floor. I hear the roar of the waves on North Beach. I hear the hatred in Alex's voice.

Where were you, Doctor, when I *really* needed you?

And you, Nietzsche, and you, Descartes, and you, Wolfgang Amadeus Mozart? You were quick enough to criticize me when you thought I was falling short of your standards. Come to me now, and tell me it's all OK, that you have messages for me about truth and beauty, right and wrong, love and hate.

There is no response. Only some thoughts:

I am a decent person.

Nice people can make mistakes.

Life is a never-ending stream of change.

And what is wrong with that?

*

When Julian gets back, he asks me how I'm feeling.

"Better," I reply.

"Good." He pauses. "Would you care to join me for dinner this evening?"

"That's awfully kind… But I feel I'm imposing on you."

"Well you are, but I seem to be enjoying the experience." He smiles. A really winning smile. Could I…? No. Not that again.

"This isn't some pick-up routine, by the way," he goes on. "I'm very happily living with a man twice my age. That's him in the photo, in the middle of the group – the one with the particularly stupid expression."

"He looks nice."

"He is, really. But don't tell him I said that."

Julian gives me his address, and I say I'll be there at 7.00.

As I walk out past the old inscription, I have no lump in my throat, just relief in my heart. Here's my KNOWLEDGE: it's time to say goodbye to Philosophy and Great Art. Let Descartes have his unique, logical point of certainty. Let Nietzsche have his authentic, self-validating inner life-force. Let Wolfgang Amadeus Mozart have his hotline to the transcendent. Me? I am an accountant/office-manager. No, I don't have permanent employment right now, but that will change; I'm good at these things. I live alone in a 'mobile home' in an end-of-the-line fenland town, but I live; I am not a bloated corpse floating face-down in the North Sea. I'm seeing a therapist for depression, but the therapy is working. I caused accidental damage to a valuable old violin, but I'm paying it off, every penny, because it is the right thing to do, not because I had packs of lawyers chasing after me.

This is who I really am. These are the selves I must be true to.

Suddenly even the exhaust-filled air of Waldram Park Road has a touch of spring to it. There's devil-may-care in my stride as I walk up to the bus stop. Bang on cue, a big red double-decker appears.

It's a 197. No use; to get back to the guest house I need a 28B.

I jump on. I must have one last try.

*

Passing the house with the skip, I tell myself that the owner has had the courage, intelligence and energy to throw the old contents away. Throw away, Stella, not cling on to. Look at that desk. It's quite nice, but it's been chucked, because the inhabitants of 62 Somersham Road have got a better one. That's what change means.

I walk on to number 38 and knock.

Silence.

Of course there is.

Well, I had to give it a go.

I turn, and head back down the street to my new life, which is my old life minus illusions.

There's a rattling noise behind me. The door of number 38 opens a crack. A beaky face peers out, as wizened as an old apple and with a deeply suspicious expression, but still unmistakably…

"Dr Licht?" I ask.

"Who are you?"

"I'm… one of your former pupils. Stella."

He shows no sign of recognition. Well, of course not. It was two decades ago. He looks about to shut the door.

"I just wanted to come round and say…" I'm suddenly aware I have no idea what I want to say. Then I do. "Thank you. Thank you for opening doors for me. I'm afraid I didn't use the doors at all well, but that was my fault – well, I didn't do anything outrageously bad, just made a bit of a bish of things. But they were my mistakes, so I'm proud of them really, because they've been part of making me who I am, and because – "

"*Sind sie Deutsch?*" he interrupts.

"Deutsch? No. *Nein. Ich bin* Stella. *Eine von…* One of your pupils."

"Pupils?"

"The… Enlightenment Club."

His eyes light up. "Ah! Quick!"

A bony hand grabs mine and pulls me in. I step over piles of junk mail and local free newspapers. A stench hits me, of rotten food and urine.

The Doctor flicks a light switch – I notice his other hand is clumsily bandaged – but no light goes on. "You're very brave," he says. "Coming here. Von Schirach has spies everywhere."

He clears some books off a chair and gestures for me to

sit down. I suddenly feel desperate for something to say, then notice in the corner –

"That old tape recorder! You played us music on it."

Licht shakes his head. "It's broken. Long ago."

"Oh. So you've got everything on CD, now?"

"CD?"

"Do you have any means of listening to music at all?"

"I know all the tunes." He begins to la the opening bars of the *Requiem*, conducting himself at the same time, then asks, "Can I make you some tea?"

"That would be lovely. But why don't I do it?"

"No! The kitchen is untidy." He shuffles across to the same door he strode over to twenty years ago. As he opens it, I spot crockery piled up beside a sink; an overflowing waste-bin and a bowl of fruit covered in grey fur.

*

It's time to go.

"So, see you tomorrow at 10," I say. I'll be back with some proper cleaning materials.

"Yes, yes. It's very kind of you."

"Not at all. We Enlightenment Club members must stick together."

"True. True."

At the door, he holds out his uninjured hand. I take it and squeeze it; he tries to squeeze back and half-succeeds.

*

Julian and I do all we can to find if Stanislas has any family in the UK. No joy. I speak to Social Services, and a stream of different individuals comes to look after him for the odd half hour a day – when he will let them in. I start visiting at weekends, doing a bit of cleaning, dusting the shelves and shelves of books (reading them in the breaks, of course), shopping, cooking, showing him *again* how to use the CD player I bought him, checking that he's eating properly and is taking his pills. During the week, Julian pops round the odd evening. As a result Stanislas seems much better: a lot of the time he's quite 'with it'. But that won't last, of course.

I talk to him about trying a home: panic fills his eyes, and he starts talking about people who vanished in 1938.

"They never came back, you know," he says.

I stay with Julian over these weekends. He has a big house that his mother left him. He and Bill let me clear out an attic and stick a bed in there, after which Bill calls me Mrs Rochester. At first, I do a bit of stuff around the place to feel better about all this hospitality – but in the end, I insist on paying him something, after which Julian says I might as well move in.

I hand back the keys to 57 Sunny View Park with pure pleasure, though I do feel a twinge of loss as we drive back through the Fens (Julian has hired a van and is helping me move). But my future is no longer in Ingelow. There are plenty of lively small businesses in busy South London looking for good, permanent accountant/office-managers.

Once a month, I go back to see Louisa. On one visit, she says I should do some writing and 'get my story out'. I'd find it deeply therapeutic, apparently. After that, I spend a couple of evenings in Mrs R's attic staring at an old notepad and don't even know where to begin.

There's no point. It's old stuff.

Over. Done. History. All of it.

Music Every Nite

It's summer. Proper summer, too, with real sun and real heat. I'm walking home – how nice to use that word and to mean it again – from the Doctor's. I suddenly feel thirsty; I'm passing a pub and suddenly think 'Why not?'

Because mother said nice women don't go into pubs on their own.

Inside, the place is dull rather than rough. The only thing I actively dislike is the landlord's spelling: *Music Every Nite*, it says on a board behind the bar. I run my eyes idly down the list of performers.

On Tuesday 24th, the featured act is The Jeff McFadden Band.

*

I ask Julian to come with me but he says he can't stand ageing rock bands. Bill can't stand rock bands of any age.

I'll go on my own, then.

"It'll be appallingly loud," says Bill.

"I'll bring a roll of supersoft loo paper to stick in my ears."

"It's a grotty pub," says Julian.

"Fine, I won't buy a Versace outfit."

"It'll be heaving with forty-something former punks with beer bellies, pretending that it's still nineteen seventy – whenever punk was."

"1976. Look, I'm going, OK?"

I turn up at 8.00, the scheduled start. There's gear on the stage but no musicians yet. I order a glass of white wine. I take a sip. Maybe I'll have the red next time. Then a man with not too much of a beer belly walks up to the bar and takes the seat next to me. Suddenly I'm desperate to tell him about 1976.

He catches my eye. "Jane?"

"No."

"Oh, I'm so sorry. I'm supposed to be meeting someone called Jane."

I nod. The conversation should end here. But I want to talk. "So, you're a punk at heart, then…" I begin.

"No. I hate punk. All that swearing." He makes a kind of sucking noise through his teeth. "I didn't realize it was going to be that sort of stuff. They normally have quite decent music here."

A woman approaches us. This is probably Jane: I never find out, as the lights go down and a man strides onto the stage, Fender Telecaster in hand. I recognize him at once, though he's ditched the 1976 gear (except for a small silver ring in his left ear) for a check shirt and denims. It suits him. Three others follow: a bassist, a drummer and a keyboard player.

Jeff walks up to his mike. "Good evening, everybody. Thanks for coming along. We'd like to start with a number called *Falling*. It's about love, and how it can go wrong and," he gives a shrug, "all that sort of stuff."

The keyboards begin with some swirling chords, then the guitar cuts in, decisive and rhythmical but not a machine gun any more. Energy, not rage. Jeff starts to sing. I'd forgotten what a good voice he has: deep and full of emotion. The bassist puts in harmonies for the second verse, then the keyboard-player makes it three-part for the chorus. It's thought-out and measured in a way that the Fuckwits never were, but it still has some of the old band's… I don't know.

What's the word?

Anyway, I'm captivated. Once a few people have ventured onto the space in front of the stage to shake their bodies about (rather half-heartedly, I feel), I join them and dance. Why not?

The more I dance, the more beautiful the music becomes. It surrounds me; it lifts me; it tells me that life is full of beauty and purpose, and that I've always known that really. I love music so much! Why has it ended up hurting me?

Then it is over.

Jeff sits at the front of the stage, selling CDs and chatting. The queue isn't exactly long, but it is slow, as he likes to chat. But finally it is my turn.

"Nice moves," he says, giving me a smile.

"Thank you." I pause. "Don't you remember me, Jeff?"

He thinks for a moment, then his eyes widen with pleasure. "Oh, my God! Lucy!"

"It's Stella, actually."

"Oh, Stella, forgive me. It's been a long time. What are you up to?"

"Working. Divorced. Short of cash," I say, then realize what a miserable old bag I sound. "But I'm fine, really. How about you?"

"About the same, actually."

"Gosh, I thought you and Annie…"

He grimaces. "It didn't work out. Too much time on the road. It takes a special kind of person to live with a working musician."

"I'm… sorry."

"These things happen." He grins. "I've got my music. I'm fine, too."

"The music's… really good."

"Not quite the old stuff, eh?"

"No. But it's still got… oomph."

He smiles. "I haven't heard anyone use that word since – well, you last used it. You're one of a kind, Stella, you really are."

I find myself blushing and ask what happened to the rest of the band.

"Tel went back to driving lorries. He still plays a bit – country and western I think he does now. Earl did a degree in Media Studies. Then he gave up drugs. Now he's my local councillor. Keeps telling me I should vote Liberal Democrat."

"You're still in touch with him? After that… argument?"

He shrugs. "I saw a lot worse in Belfast. How is Lucy?"

"She's engaged to a rich American. They live in LA. Los Angeles."

"I do know where LA is, Stella."

"Sorry, I…"

Jeff is grinning, and I find myself grinning too.

"Lucy and I chat on the phone," I tell him. "But… It's a different world."

He nods. "And what about Stella? Tell me more."

"Well, I… I'm just me, really."

"Best thing to be. Come on; give us a hand with this speaker and I'll get you a drink."

*

Jeff offers to take me home in his white Transit van. "It's OK. I'm legal now," he says.

"That would be nice," I reply.

"Good." He scrabbles around for CDs – he really needs someone to tidy this vehicle up – then finds one and puts it on. "Wolfie's flute concerto in G. I'm learning it properly this time. Still can't do all the twiddly bits, but I'll get there."

We arrive at my house – well, 'my house' is how it feels. I ask him in, but he says he doesn't leave gear parked in the street. I say I'll see him at the gig he's been telling me about, next week at a pub in Hackney. He replies that if I turn up, he'll play *Moon River* for me. I say I won't miss it for the world.

He leans fractionally towards me, and I lean towards him, too, and offer him a cheek to kiss. It just feels the right thing to do. He does so, very graciously.

Haunting

"I've fallen in love!" I tell Julian a few days later.

"That's good."

"I don't know. My track record on that is… well, you know all about that." He does. "We've only just met. Or re-met."

"He's not an avant-garde composer with a bit of a reputation as a seducer/ditcher, is he?"

"Not… avant-garde. But he does write songs."

"Ah. I thought you looked cheerful the other evening. There was a spring in your step."

"Was I that obvious?"

"Subtlety is not your strong point, Stella. Thank God."

"So what should I do?"

"You know what you must do. Follow your heart. Try not to smash whatever it is he plays, though."

"No… Oh, Julian, that's what I'm afraid of. Supposing he finds out about what happened with Alex?"

"Why should he?"

"Because I don't want secrets in our relationship."

"Everybody has secrets. Bill knows nothing about the bizarre series of murders that happened a few years back on the campus where I just happened to be teaching."

"No, seriously, Julian…"

"No, seriously, Stella. Everyone has secrets."

"I guess so…"

My mind goes back to that little room again, as it always seems to. An Enlightenment Club member should not have secrets. We have a commitment to truthfulness.

"Anyway, you don't really know he wants to get with you," Julian says. "Has he said that? I don't want to pry – no, rubbish, I'm desperate to pry – but how intimate have you been?"

"He… kissed me on the cheek in the van."

"Better start getting the engagement party organized!"

"It felt… special."

Julian nods. "I know what you mean, Stella. There are kisses and kisses, aren't there? But don't put all your bets on this. Yet."

"So what do I do about the Alex stuff?"

"You'll just have to find the right moment to tell him. Reasonably soon is my advice. Too soon and you might scare him off. Make sure he is serious, then say there are things you need to sort out."

"But the deeper I get in, the more it will hurt if he can't handle it. *The musician-staking, violin-smashing madwoman…*"

"The very pleasant and civilized woman who made a fuck-up of something a year or so ago."

We're sitting opposite each other, and I go over and give him an enormous hug.

*

The Hackney gig.

A tiny bit of me wants it to be awful, and him to look ridiculous or pretentious or – well, you know that story. He doesn't, of course. *Moon River* is lovely, his dedicating it to me embarrassing but spine-tingling.

I try not to be too obvious hanging around after the show, but Jeff simply beckons me over and starts showing me how to pack the equipment away. That could be seen as presumptuous and sexist, but I think it is kind. What else was I supposed to do?

He introduces me to the band. "Stella knows me from my punk days. I'm sure she's disappointed in me now and thinks I've sold out, but she's come along anyway…"

"No, I like your music now. All of you," I add, looking round at his colleagues. It seems important, somehow.

Then I get back to work.

"Careful with the guitar," says Jeff.

He insists on driving me home, though it's miles out of his way. Just before we reach the Rotherhithe Tunnel, he asks if I'd like to come round for dinner one evening. "I'm not exactly a *cordon bleu* cook," he adds.

I tell him I'd love to.

Then. I'll tell him then.

*

I don't.

I don't know why. There just never seems to be a moment. It's such a lovely evening. I don't want to spoil it.

Over breakfast?

Don't jump to conclusions – he insists on sleeping on the sofa, adding that it's a lot more comfy than a van on the M1.

*

So tell him at my reciprocal dinner, where I invite him to meet Julian and Bill.

(Again, another get-out: he'll turn out to be homophobic. End of dilemma. He isn't, of course. "Lovely guys," he says in the hall afterwards, where we have such a nice cuddle.)

"You really ought to tell him soon," Julian says the next day. "Soon or not at all. Ever."

"No, I couldn't do 'not at all'. It would be wrong.

Deceitful. And he might find out! Imagine how awful that would be!"

*

We actually go to bed after the fourth gig. It's so lovely, so unpressured, so simply joyful.

"I love you," I tell him afterwards, and he smiles.

"That's mutual, Stella. I think you're the oddest woman I have ever met. Truly odd, not just weird for the hell of it – there are loads of them around. No disrespect, but your sister was a bit like that. Good fun, but… You're so much more… substantial."

"You mean fat," I say jokingly.

"That too," he says, squeezing a bit of my tummy and giving a charmingly naughty smile. "But you know what I mean."

"I do, Jeff. And I accept your compliment. From the bottom of my heart."

"That means a lot, my beautiful, strange, special Stella!"

This, surely, is the moment.

But it feels so nice as it is!

"Any dark secrets I should know about?" he asks.

I start shaking my head.

Oh, Stella, Stella! What are you doing?

He nods. "I have. My parents were really into this Orange Order shit. I'd even go on the Junior Order marches, God help me. Me and my mates in our crew-cuts and sashes. It was all I'd known. From mum and dad. From the lads at school. When I was fourteen, a load of us went out one evening and beat up this Catholic boy. Punched him. Kicked him. In the face. Put him in hospital. And before you say anything, I did my share of kicking. Fuck, I still think about that poor guy…"

He shakes his head, and I stroke his hair. "You were just a kid. It's… the things we've done as adults that need revealing." I'm not sure this is true – doesn't *all* inner venom need to be removed? – but it puts me at the point of no return, which is what I need.

"Well, I guess there's a few things I should – " he begins.

"No, Jeff. It's my turn."

"OK."

I tell him the whole story.

"It was an accident!" I say, far too loud, at the end.

He simply nods.

"You must believe me!" I add.

He nods again.

He's appalled. That's it. Over.

"Of course I believe you," he says. "Why shouldn't I? The whole thing is very you, Stella. The big deep river. Now with dangerous currents. As I always suspected."

"Always?"

"I've met smiling old men who turn out to have been terrorists. Singers who are bursting with love on stage and complete bitches off it. Earl, for fuck's sake. He's a total arse, but I can't help liking him really. I don't trust obvious people, Stella. Never have. I trust people like you, who make really stupid mistakes but then have the integrity to face up to them. Come here…"

He puts his arms around me, and I feel enfolded, understood, truly loving and loved for who I really am, awfulness and all, for the first time in my life.

A Few Years Later

A weird thing happened the other day…

We're doing a festival. I love festivals, little closed worlds where people are united by a passion for music (OK, and a passion for drink and drugs at some of them, but the nicest ones aren't like that…) Anyway, this is a really pleasant one, in a couple of fields just north of London. Jeff is playing on the second stage, which is for original acts; the main one is for 'tribute' bands, who play other people's material, which is what the audience likes best.

Jeff is in a couple of such bands himself, one creating the Golden Era of Rock'n'Roll (of which he has no memory) and another called Super Smooth Sounds of the Seventies (no punk, then). He enjoys them – "You can do anything well or badly," he says – but I know he's happiest on the smaller stage playing his own compositions to a handful of people who really feel them. Lots of our friends are like that: 'commercial' gigs to subsidize the original work.

We get by. I'm very much part-time now. Mainly because of the little girl sitting beside me, in an earnest discussion with a one-eared ragdoll called Pooks. But also because of my degree (also part time, of course). Not in philosophy – the department at Catford is still obsessed with language games – but anthropology. Julian's suggestion, and a brilliant one. My tutor, who spent several years in the Amazon basin and was nearly killed in a set-to with another group (we don't use the word 'tribe'), says I have a 'real flair' for it.

The guys do their set, very well, I think. The new drummer is fitting in: he was a little overfussy at first, doing fills at every possible opportunity, but now he is properly behind the music. Jeff is busy with his usual debrief, so I take Lizzie-Louise off to see the 'main' act.

A big purple and silver banner across the front of the stage proclaims them as ABBATABULOUS!, and they're playing *Take a Chance on Me*. Two lady singers, maybe getting a *little* old for this, dressed, if not to kill, to impose life-changing injuries. A guitarist with a star-shaped guitar (Björn's original, according to Jeff, was handmade). Bass. Drums. And on keyboards…

It can't be!

It is.

I feel a sudden dizziness. I'm back on the doorstep of 26 Common Road, Cawston. I'm facing the roaring waves of Ingelow North Beach. Any guilt I felt about damaging Alex's violin has long been washed away (the sight of most of my divorce settlement, when it finally arrived, disappearing into paying off the loan was particularly therapeutic). But I suddenly feel overwhelmed with questions I want to ask him. Does he still think I smashed it deliberately? Did the replacement really cost £20,000? What happened to that concerto? Who was that woman I saw him shopping with? Are they still together? I must know!

"I like this!" says Lizzie-Louise, pulling me towards the stage. I let her – then suddenly see Alex look up from his keyboard and scan the audience. I don't think he is searching for anyone in particular; it's just something to do. He certainly doesn't notice me.

Next time he might. I pull down my big straw hat – it had a plume, but it fell out while I was helping set up – and turn round. "It's… a bit loud," I say.

"Daddy's loud."

"I haven't got my ear protectors. Nor have you."

"My ears don't mind."

"Well I do. Come on, Lizzie-Lou. Daddy's waiting."

"What for?"

I haul her back and she glares at me, a fully paid-up member of Toddlers Against Bossy Parents. I glance at the stage again. Alex is scowling, now. Was 'Agnetha' slightly off key? Yes – ouch, she's done it again – but I know that scowl. It's more than a bum note or three. Much, much more.

Suddenly I feel terribly sorry for him, in a way I never have before.

My bolshy, almost unbearably beautiful daughter tugs at my hand, but we must go. Now.

I haven't got time for that old stuff.

THE END

Thank you for reading this story. I hope you enjoyed it.

If you did, I'd be very grateful if you would say so on amazon or goodreads. And do visit my website and/or get in touch: chris@chriswest.info

If you hated it, sorry. No book can please everyone, or should try to.

Either way, happy reading in the future!

Chris

Printed in Great Britain
by Amazon

47602449R00108